THE KING OF ELFLAND'S DAUGHTER

By LORD DUNSANY

The King of Elfland's Daughter
By Lord Dunsany

Print ISBN 13: 978-1-4209-7838-4
eBook ISBN 13: 978-1-4209-7973-2

This edition copyright © 2021. Digireads.com Publishing.

Cover Image: a detail of the frontispiece by S. H. Sime, published by G. P. Putnam's Sons, New York, c. 1924.

Please visit *www.digireads.com*

TO

LADY DUNSANY

Preface

I hope that no suggestion of any strange land that may be conveyed by the title will scare readers away from this book; for, though some chapters do indeed tell of Elfland, in the greater part of them there is no more to be shown than the face of the fields we know, and ordinary English woods and a common village and valley, a good twenty or twenty-five miles from the border of Elfland.

LORD DUNSANY

Chapter I

The Plan of the Parliament of Erl

In their ruddy jackets of leather that reached to their knees the men of Erl appeared before their lord, the stately white-haired man in his long red room. He leaned in his carven chair and heard their spokesman.

And thus their spokesman said.

"For seven hundred years the chiefs of your race have ruled us well; and their deeds are remembered by the minor minstrels, living on yet in their little tinkling songs. And yet the generations stream away, and there is no new thing."

"What would you?" said the lord.

"We would be ruled by a magic lord," they said.

"So be it," said the lord. "It is five hundred years since my people have spoken thus in parliament, and it shall always be as your parliament saith. You have spoken. So be it."

And he raised his hand and blessed them and they went. *given magic*

They went back to their ancient crafts, to the fitting of iron to the hooves of horses, to working upon leather, to tending flowers, to ministering to the rugged needs of Earth; they followed the ancient ways, and looked for a new thing. But the old lord sent a word to his eldest son, bidding him come before him.

And very soon the young man stood before him, in that same carven chair from which he had not moved, where light, growing late, from high windows, showed the aged eyes looking far into the future beyond that old lord's time. And seated there he gave his son his commandment.

"Go forth," he said, "before these days of mine are over, and therefore go in haste, and go from here eastwards and pass the fields we know, till you see the lands that clearly pertain to faery; and cross their boundary, which is made of twilight, and come to that palace that is only told of in song."

"It is far from here," said the young man Alveric.

"Yes," answered he, "it is far."

"And further still," the young man said, "to return. For distances in those fields are not as here."

"Even so," said his father.

"What do you bid me do," said the son, "when I come to that palace?"

And his father said: "To wed the King of Elfland's daughter."

The young man thought of her beauty and crown of ice, and the sweetness that fabulous runes had told was hers. Songs were sung of her on wild hills where tiny strawberries grew, at dusk and by early starlight, and if one sought the singer no man was there. Sometimes only her name was sung softly over and over. Her name was Lirazel.

She was a princess of the magic line. The gods had sent their shadows to her christening, and the fairies too would have gone, but that they were frightened to see on their dewy fields the long dark moving shadows of the gods, so they stayed hidden in crowds of pale pink anemones, and thence blessed Lirazel.

"My people demand a magic lord to rule over them. They have chosen foolishly," the old lord said, "and only the Dark Ones that show not their faces know all that this will bring: but we, who see not, follow the ancient custom and do what our people in their parliament say. It may be some spirit of wisdom they have not known may save them even yet. Go then with your face turned towards that light that beats from fairyland, and that faintly illumines the dusk between sunset and early stars, and this shall guide you till you come to the frontier and have passed the fields we know."

Then he unbuckled a strap and a girdle of leather and gave his huge sword to his son, saying: "This that has brought our family down the ages unto this day shall surely guard you always upon your journey, even though you fare beyond the fields we know."

And the young man took it though he knew that no such sword could avail him.

Near the Castle of Erl there lived a lonely witch, on high land near the thunder, which used to roll in Summer along the hills. There she dwelt by herself in a narrow cottage of thatch and roamed the high fields alone to gather the thunderbolts. Of these thunderbolts, that had no earthly forging, were made, with suitable runes, such weapons as had to parry unearthly dangers.

And alone would roam this witch at certain tides of Spring, taking the form of a young girl in her beauty, singing among tall flowers in gardens of Erl. She would go at the hour when hawk-moths first pass from bell to bell. And of those few that had seen her was this son of the Lord of Erl. And though it was calamity to love her, though it rapt men's thoughts away from all things true, yet the beauty of the form that was not hers had lured him to gaze at her with deep young eyes, till—whether flattery or pity moved her, who knows that is mortal?— she spared him whom her arts might well have destroyed and, changing instantly in that garden there, showed him the rightful form of a deadly witch. And even then his eyes did not at once forsake her, and in the moments that his glance still lingered upon that withered shape that haunted the hollyhocks he had her gratitude that may not be bought, nor won by any charms that Christians know. And she had beckoned to him and he had followed, and learned from her on her thunder-haunted hill that on the day of need a sword might be made of metals not sprung from Earth, with runes along it that would waft away, certainly any thrust of earthly sword, and except for three master-runes could thwart the weapons of Elfland.

As he took his father's sword the young man thought of the witch.

It was scarcely dark in the valley when he left the Castle of Erl, and went so swiftly up the witch's hill that a dim light lingered yet on its highest heaths when he came near the cottage of the one that he sought, and found her burning bones at a fire in the open. To her he said that the day of his need was come. And she bade him gather thunderbolts in her garden, in the soft earth under her cabbages.

And there with eyes that saw every minute more dimly, and fingers that grew accustomed to the thunderbolts' curious surfaces, he found before darkness came down on him seventeen: and these he heaped into a silken kerchief and carried back to the witch.

On the grass beside her he laid those strangers to Earth. From wonderful spaces they came to her magical garden, shaken by thunder from paths that we cannot tread; and though not in themselves containing magic were well adapted to carry what magic her runes could give. She laid the thigh-bone of a materialist down, and turned to those stormy wanderers. She arranged them in one straight row by the side of her fire. And over them then she toppled the burning logs and the embers, prodding them down with the ebon stick that is the sceptre of witches, until she had deeply covered those seventeen cousins of Earth that had visited us from their etherial home. She stepped back then from her fire and stretched out her hands, and suddenly blasted it with a frightful rune. The flames leaped up in amazement. And what had been but a lonely fire in the night, with no more mystery than pertains to all such fires, flared suddenly into a thing that wanderers feared.

As the green flames, stung by her runes, leaped up, and the heat of the fire grew intenser, she stepped backwards further and further, and merely uttered her runes a little louder the further she got from the fire. She bade Alveric pile on logs, dark logs of oak that lay there cumbering the heath; and at once, as he dropped them on, the heat licked them up; and the witch went on pronouncing her louder runes, and the flames danced wild and green; and down in the embers the seventeen, whose paths had once crossed Earth's when they wandered free, knew heat again as great as they had known, even on that desperate ride that had brought them here. And when Alveric could no longer come near the fire, and the witch was some yards from it shouting her runes, the magical flames burned all the ashes away and that portent that flared on the hill as suddenly ceased, leaving only a circle that sullenly glowed on the ground, like the evil pool that glares where thermite has burst. And flat in the glow, all liquid still, lay the sword.

The witch approached it and pared its edges with a sword that she drew from her thigh. Then she sat down beside it on the earth and sang to it while it cooled. Not like the runes that enraged the flames was the song she sang to the sword: she whose curses had blasted the fire till it shrivelled big logs of oak crooned now a melody like a wind in summer blowing from wild wood gardens that no man tended, down valleys loved once by children, now lost to them but for dreams, a song of such memories as lurk and hide along the edges of oblivion, now flashing from beautiful years of glimpse of some golden moment, now passing swiftly out of remembrance again, to go back to the shades of oblivion, and leaving on the mind those faintest traces of little shining feet which when dimly perceived by us are called regrets. She sang of old Summer noons in the time of harebells: she sang on that high dark heath a song that seemed so full of mornings and evenings preserved with all their dews by her magical craft from days that had else been lost, that Alveric wondered of each small wandering wing, that her fire had lured from the dusk, if this were the ghost of some day lost to man, called up by the force of her song from times that were fairer. And all the while the unearthly metal grew harder. The white liquid stiffened and turned red. The glow of the red dwindled. And as it cooled it narrowed: little particles came together, little crevices closed: and as they closed they seized the air about them, and with the air they caught the witch's rune, and gripped it and held it forever. And so it was it became a magical sword. And little magic there is in English woods, from the time of anemones to the falling of leaves, that was not in the sword. And little magic there is in southern downs, that only sheep roam over and quiet shepherds, that the sword had not too. And there was scent of thyme in it and sight of lilac, and the chorus of birds that sings before dawn in April, and the deep proud splendour of rhododendrons, and the litheness and laughter of streams, and miles and miles of may. And by the time the sword was black it was all enchanted with magic.

Nobody can tell you about that sword all that there is to be told of it; for those that know of those paths of Space on which its metals once floated, till Earth caught them one by one as she sailed past on her orbit, have little time to waste on such things as magic, and so cannot tell you how the sword was made, and those who know whence poetry is, and the need that man has for song, or know any one of the fifty branches of magic, have little time to waste on such things as science, and so cannot tell you whence its ingredients came. Enough that it was once beyond our Earth and was now here amongst our mundane stones; that it was once but as those stones, and now had something in it such as soft music has; let those that can define it.

And now the witch drew the black blade forth by the hilt, which was thick and on one side rounded, for she had cut a small groove in the soil below the hilt for this purpose, and began to sharpen both sides of the sword by rubbing them with a curious greenish stone, still singing over the sword an eerie song.

Alveric watched her in silence, wondering, not counting time; it may have been for moments, it may have been while the stars went far on their courses. Suddenly she was finished. She stood up with the sword lying on both her hands. She stretched it out curtly to Alveric; he took it, she turned away; and there was a look in her eyes as though she would have kept that sword, or kept Alveric. He turned to pour out his thanks, but she was gone.

He rapped on the door of the dark house; he called "Witch, Witch" along the lonely heath, till children heard on far farms and were terrified. Then he turned home, and that was best for him.

Chapter II

Alveric Comes in Sight of the Elfin Mountains

To the long chamber, sparsely furnished, high in a tower, in which Alveric slept, there came a ray direct from the rising sun. He awoke, and remembered at once the magical sword, which made all his awaking joyous. It is natural to feel glad at the thought of a recent gift, but there was also a certain joy in the sword itself, which perhaps could communicate with Alveric's thoughts all the more easily just as they came from dreamland, which was pre-eminently the sword's own country; but, however it be, all those that have come by a magical sword, have always felt that joy while it still was new, clearly and unmistakably.

He had no farewells to make, but thought it better instantly to obey his father's command than to stay to explain why he took upon his adventure a sword that he deemed to be better than the one his father loved. So he stayed not even to eat, but put food in a wallet and slung

over him by a strap a bottle of good new leather, not waiting to fill it
for he knew he should meet with streams; and, wearing his father's
sword as swords are commonly worn, he slung the other over his back
with its rough hilt tied near his shoulder, and strode away from the
Castle and Vale of Erl. Of money he took but little, half a handful of
copper only, for use in the fields we know; for he knew not what coin
or what means of exchange were used on the other side of the frontier
of twilight.

Now the Vale of Erl is very near to the border beyond which there
is none of the fields we know. He climbed the hill and strode over the
fields and passed through woods of hazel; and the blue sky shone on
him merrily as he went by the way of the fields, and the blue was as
bright by his feet when he came to the woods, for it was the time of the
bluebells. He ate, and filled his water-bottle, and travelled all day
eastwards, and at evening the mountains of faery came floating into
view, the colour of pale forget-me-nots.

As the sun set behind Alveric he looked at those pale-blue
mountains to see with what colour their peaks would astonish the
evening; but never a tint they took from the setting sun, whose
splendour was gilding all the fields we know, never a wrinkle faded
upon their precipices, never a shadow deepened, and Alveric learned
that for nothing that happens here is any change in the enchanted lands.

He turned his eyes from their serene pale beauty back to the fields
we know. And there, with their gables lifting into the sunlight above
deep hedgerows beautiful with Spring, he saw the cottages of earthly
men. Past them he walked while the beauty of evening grew, with
songs of birds, and scents wandering from flowers, and odours that
deepened and deepened, and evening decked herself to receive the
Evening Star. But before that star appeared the young adventurer found
the cottage he sought; for, flapping above its doorway, he saw the sign
of huge brown hide with outlandish letters in gilt which proclaimed the
dweller below to be a worker in leather.

An old man came to the door when Alveric knocked, little and bent
with age, and he bent more when Alveric named himself. And the
young man asked for a scabbard for his sword, yet said not what sword
it was. And they both went into the cottage where the old wife was, by
her big fire, and the couple did honour to Alveric. The old man then sat
down near his thick table, whose surface shone with smoothness
wherever it was not pitted by little tools that had drilled through pieces
of leather all that man's lifetime and in the times of his fathers. And
then he laid the sword upon his knees and wondered at the roughness of
hilt and guard, for they were raw unworked metal, and at the huge
width of the sword; and then he screwed up his eyes and began to think
of his trade. And in a while he thought out what must be done; and his
wife brought him a fine hide; and he marked out on it two pieces as

wide as the sword, and a bit wider than that.

And any questions he asked concerning that wide bright sword Alveric somewhat parried, for he wished not to perplex his mind by telling him all that it was: he perplexed that old couple enough a little later when he asked them for lodging for the night. And this they gave him with as many apologies as if it were they that had asked a favour, and gave him a great supper out of their cauldron, in which boiled everything that the old man snared; but nothing that Alveric was able to say prevented them giving up their bed to him and preparing a heap of skins for their own night's rest by the fire.

And after their supper the old man cut out the two wide pieces of leather with a point at the end of each and began to stitch them together on each side. And then Alveric began to ask him of the way, and the old leather-worker spoke of North and South and West and even of north-east, but of East or south-east he spoke never a word. He dwelt near the very edge of the fields we know, yet of any hint of anything lying beyond them he or his wife said nothing. Where Alveric's journey lay upon the morrow they seemed to think the world ended.

And pondering afterwards, in the bed they gave him, all that the old man had said, Alveric sometimes marvelled at his ignorance, and yet sometimes wondered if it might have been skill by which those two had avoided all the evening any word of anything lying to the East or south-east of their home. He wondered if in his early days the old man might have gone there, but he was unable even to wonder what he had found there if he had gone. Then Alveric fell asleep, and dreams gave him hints and guesses of the old man's wanderings in Fairyland, but gave him no better guides than he had already, and these were the pale-blue peaks of the Elfin Mountains.

The old man woke him after he had slept long. When he came to the day-room a bright fire was burning there, his breakfast was ready for him and the scabbard made, which fitted the sword exactly. The old people waited on him silently and took payment for the scabbard, but would not take aught for their hospitality. Silently they watched him rise to go, and followed him without a word to the door, and outside it watched him still, clearly hoping that he would turn to the North or West; but when he turned and strode for the Elfin Mountains, they watched him no more, for their faces never were turned that way. And though they watched him no longer yet he waved his hand in farewell; for he had a feeling for the cottages and fields of these simple folk, such as they had not for the enchanted lands. He walked in the sparkling morning through scenes familiar from infancy; he saw the ruddy orchis flowering early, reminding the bluebells they were just past their prime; the small young leaves of the oak were yet a brownish yellow; the new beech-leaves shone like brass, where the cuckoo was calling clearly; and a birch tree looked like a wild woodland creature that had draped herself in green gauze; on favoured bushes there were buds of may. Alveric said over and over to himself farewell to all these things: the cuckoo went on calling, and not for him. And then, as he pushed through a hedge into a field untended, there suddenly close before him in the field was, as his father had told, the frontier of twilight. It stretched across the fields in front of him, blue and dense like water; and things seen through it seemed misshapen and shining. He looked back once over the fields we know; the cuckoo went on calling unconcernedly; a small bird sang about its own affairs; and, nothing seeming to answer or heed his farewells, Alveric strode on boldly into those long masses of twilight.

A man in a field not far was calling to horses, there were folk talking in a neighbouring lane, as Alveric stepped into the rampart of twilight; at once all these sounds grew dim, humming faintly, as from great distances: in a few strides he was through, and not a murmur at all came then from the fields we know. The fields through which he had come had suddenly ended; there was no trace of its hedges bright with new green; he looked back, and the frontier seemed lowering, cloudy and smoky; he looked all round and saw no familiar thing; in the place of the beauty of May were the wonders and splendours of Elfland.

The pale-blue mountains stood august in their glory, shimmering and rippling in a golden light that seemed as though it rhythmically poured from the peaks and flooded all those slopes with breezes of gold. And below them, far off as yet, he saw going up all silver into the air the spires of the palace only told of in song. He was on a plain on which the flowers were queer and the shape of the trees monstrous. He started at once toward the silver spires.

To those who may have wisely kept their fancies within the boundary of the fields we know it is difficult for me to tell of the land to which Alveric had come, so that in their minds they can see that plain with its scattered trees and far off the dark wood out of which the palace of Elfland lifted those glittering spires, and above them and beyond them that serene range of mountains whose pinnacles took no colour from any light we see. Yet it is for this very purpose that our fancies travel far, and if my reader through fault of mine fail to picture the peaks of Elfland my fancy had better have stayed in the fields we know. Know then that in Elfland are colours more deep than are in our fields, and the very air there glows with so deep a lucency that all things seen there have something of the look of our trees and flowers in June reflected in water. And the colour of Elfland, of which I despaired to tell, may yet be told, for we have hints of it here; the deep blue of the night in Summer just as the gloaming has gone, the pale blue of Venus flooding the evening with light, the deeps of lakes in the twilight, all these are hints of that colour. And while our sunflowers carefully turned to the sun, some forefather of the rhododendrons must have turned a little towards Elfland, so that some of that glory dwells with them to this day. And, above all, our painters have had many a glimpse of that country, so that sometimes in pictures we see a glamour too wonderful for our fields; it is a memory of theirs that intruded from some old glimpse of the pale-blue mountains while they sat at easels painting the fields we know.

So Alveric strode on through the luminous air of that land whose glimpses dimly remembered are inspirations here. And at once he felt less lonely. For there is a barrier in the fields we know, drawn sharply between men and all other life, so that if we be but a day away from our kind we are lonely; but once across the boundary of twilight and Alveric saw this barrier was down. Crows walking on the moor looked whimsically at him, all manner of little creatures peered curiously to see who was come from a quarter whence so few ever came; to see who went on a journey whence so few ever returned; for the King of Elfland guarded his daughter well, as Alveric knew although he knew not how. There was a merry sparkle of interest in all those little eyes, and a look that might mean warning.

There was perhaps less mystery here than on our side of the boundary of twilight; for nothing lurked or seemed to lurk behind great boles of oak, as in certain lights and seasons things may lurk in the fields we know; no strangeness hid on the far side of ridges; nothing haunted deep woods; whatever might possibly lurk was clearly there to be seen, whatever strangeness might be was spread in full sight of the traveller, whatever might haunt deep woods lived there in the open day.

And, so strong lay the enchantment deep over all that land, that not only did beasts and men guess each other's meanings well, but there seemed to be an understanding even, that reached from men to trees and from trees to men. Lonely pine trees that Alveric passed now and then on the moor, their trunks glowing always with the ruddy light that they had got by magic from some old sunset, seemed to stand with their branches akimbo and lean over a little to look at him. It seemed almost as though they had not always been trees, before enchantment had overtaken them there; it seemed they would tell him something.

But Alveric heeded no warnings either from beasts or trees, and strode away toward the enchanted wood.

Chapter III

The Magical Sword Meets Some of the Swords of Elfland

When Alveric came to the enchanted wood the light in which Elfland glowed had neither grown nor dwindled, and he saw that it came from no radiance that shines on the fields we know, unless the wandering lights of wonderful moments that sometimes astonish our fields, and are gone the instant they come, are strayed over the border of Elfland by some momentary disorder of magic. Neither sun nor moon made the light of that enchanted day.

A line of pine trees up which ivy climbed, as high as their lowering black foliage, stood like sentinels at the edge of the wood. The silver spires were shining as though it were they that made all this azure glow in which Elfland swam. And Alveric having by now come far into Elfland, and being now before its capital palace, and knowing that Elfland guarded its mysteries well, drew his father's sword before he entered the wood. The other still hung on his back, slung in its new scabbard over his left shoulder.

And the moment he passed by one of those guardian pine trees, the ivy that lived on it unfastened its tendrils and, rapidly letting itself down, came straight for Alveric and clutched at his throat.

The long thin sword of his father was just in time; had it not been drawn he would have scarcely got it out, so swift was the rush of the ivy. He cut tendril after tendril that grasped his limbs as ivy grasps old towers, and still more tendrils came for him, until he severed its main stem between him and the tree. And as he was doing this he heard a hissing rush behind him, and another had come down from another tree and was rushing at him with all its leaves spread out. The green thing looked wild and angry as it gripped his left shoulder as though it would hold it forever. But Alveric severed those tendrils with a blow of his sword and then fought with the rest, while the first one was still alive but now too short to reach him, and was lashing its branches angrily on the ground. And soon, as the surprise of the attack was over and he had freed himself of the tendrils that had gripped him, Alveric stepped back till the ivy could not reach him and he could still fight it with his long sword. The ivy crawled back then to lure Alveric on, and sprang at him when he followed it. But, terrible though the grip of ivy is, that was a good sharp sword; and very soon Alveric, all bruised though he was, had so lopped his assailant that it fled back up its tree. Then he stepped back and looked at the wood in the light of his new experience, choosing a way through. He saw at once that in the barrier of pine trees the two in front of him had had their ivy so shortened in the fight that if he went mid-way between the two the ivy of neither would be able to reach him. He then stepped forward, but the moment he did so he noticed one of the pine trees move closer to the other. He knew then that the time was come to draw his magical sword.

So he returned his father's sword to the scabbard by his side and drew out the other over his shoulder and, going straight up to the tree that had moved, swept at the ivy as it sprang at him: and the ivy fell all at once to the ground, not lifeless but a heap of common ivy. And then he gave one blow to the trunk of the tree, and a chip flew out not larger than a common sword would have made, but the whole tree shuddered;

and with that shudder disappeared at once a certain ominous look that the pine had had, and it stood there an ordinary unenchanted tree. Then he stepped on through the wood with his sword drawn.

He had not gone many paces when he heard behind him a sound like a faint breeze in the tree-tops, yet no wind was blowing in that wood at all. He looked round therefore, and saw that the pine trees were following him. They were coming slowly after him, keeping well out of the way of his sword, but to left and right they were gaining on him, so that he saw he was being gradually shut in by a crescent that grew thicker and thicker as it crowded amongst the trees that it met on the way, and would soon crush him to death. Alveric saw at once that to turn back would be fatal, and decided to push right on, relying chiefly on speed; for his quick perception had already noticed something slow about the magic that swayed the wood; as though whoever controlled it were old or weary of magic, or interrupted by other things. So he went straight ahead, hitting every tree in his way, whether enchanted or not, a blow with his magical sword; and the runes that ran in that metal from the other side of the sun were stronger than any spells that there were in the wood. Great oak trees with sinister boles drooped and lost all their enchantment as Alveric flashed past them with a flick of that magical sword. He was marching faster than the clumsy pines. And soon he left in that weird and eerie wood a wake of trees that were wholly unenchanted, that stood there now without hint of romance or mystery even.

And all of a sudden he came from the gloom of the wood to the emerald glory of the Elf King's lawns. Again, we have hints of such things here. Imagine lawns of ours just emerging from night, flashing early lights from their dewdrops when all the stars have gone; bordered with flowers that just begin to appear, their gentle colours all coming back after night; untrodden by any feet except the tiniest and wildest; shut off from the wind and the world by trees in whose fronds is still darkness: picture these waiting for the birds to sing; there is almost a hint there sometimes of the glow of the lawns of Elfland; but then it passes so quickly that we can never be sure. More beautiful than aught our wonder guesses, more than our hearts have hoped, were the dewdrop lights and twilights in which these lawns glowed and shone. And we have another thing by which to hint of them, those seaweeds or sea-mosses that drape Mediterranean rocks and shine out of blue-green water for gazers from dizzy cliffs: more like sea-floors were these lawns than like any land of ours, for the air of Elfland is thus deep and blue.

At the beauty of these lawns Alveric stood gazing as they shone through twilight and dew, surrounded by the mauve and ruddy glory of the massed flowers of Elfland, beside which our sunsets pale and our orchids droop; and beyond them lay like night the magical wood. And jutting from that wood, with glittering portals all open wide to the lawns, with windows more blue than our sky on Summer's nights; as though built of starlight; shone that palace that may be only told of in song.

As Alveric stood there with his sword in his hand, at the wood's edge, scarcely breathing, with his eyes looking over the lawns at the chiefest glory of Elfland; through one of the portals alone came the King of Elfland's daughter. She walked dazzling to the lawns without seeing Alveric. Her feet brushed through the dew and the heavy air and gently pressed for an instant the emerald grass, which bent and rose, as our harebells when blue butterflies light and leave them, roaming carefree along the hills of chalk.

And as she passed he neither breathed nor moved, nor could have moved if those pines had still pursued him, but they stayed in the forest not daring to touch those lawns.

She wore a crown that seemed to be carved of great pale sapphires; she shone on those lawns and gardens like a dawn coming unaware, out of long night, on some planet nearer than us to the sun. And as she passed near Alveric she suddenly turned her head; and her eyes opened in a little wonder. She had never before seen a man from the fields we know.

And Alveric gazed in her eyes all speechless and powerless still: it was indeed the Princess Lirazel in her beauty. And then he saw that her crown was not of sapphires but ice.

"Who are you?" she said. And her voice had the music that, of earthly things, was most like ice in thousands of broken pieces rocked by a wind of Spring upon lakes in some northern country.

And he said: "I come from the fields that are mapped and known."

And then she sighed for a moment for those fields, for she had heard how life beautifully passes there, and how there are always in those fields young generations, and she thought of the changing seasons and children and age, of which elfin minstrels had sung when they told of Earth.

And when he saw her sigh for the fields we know he told her somewhat of that land whence he had come. And she questioned him further, and soon he was telling her tales of his home and the Vale of Erl. And she wondered to hear of it and asked him many questions more; and then he told her all that he knew of Earth, not presuming to tell Earth's story from what his own eyes had seen in his bare score of years, but telling those tales and fables of the ways of beasts and men, that the folk of Erl had drawn out of the ages, and which their elders told by the fire at evening when children asked of what happened long ago. Thus on the edge of those lawns whose miraculous glory was framed by flowers we have never known, with the magical wood behind them, and that palace shining near which may only be told of in song, they spoke of the simple wisdom of old men and old women, telling of harvests and the blossoming of roses and may, of when to plant in gardens, of what wild animals knew; how to heal, how to sow, how to thatch, and of which of the winds in what seasons blow over the fields we know.

And then there appeared those knights who guard that palace lest any should come through the enchanted wood. Four of them they came shining over the lawns in armour, their faces not to be seen. In all the enchanted centuries of their lives they had not dared to dream of the princess: they had never bared their faces when they knelt armed before her. Yet they had sworn an oath of dreadful words that no man else should ever speak with her, if one should come through the enchanted wood. With this oath now on their lips they marched towards Alveric.

Lirazel looked at them sorrowfully yet could not halt them, for they came by command of her father which she could not avert; and well she knew that her father might not recall his command, for he had uttered it ages ago at the bidding of Fate. Alveric looked at their armour, which seemed to be brighter than any metal of ours, as though it came from one of those buttresses near, which are only told of in song; then he went towards them drawing his father's sword, for he thought to drive its slender point through some joint of the armour. The other he put into his left hand.

As the first knight struck, Alveric parried, and stopped the blow, but there came a shock like lightning into his arm and the sword flew from his hand, and he knew that no earthly sword could meet the weapons of Elfland, and took the magical sword in his right hand. With this he parried the strokes of the Princess Lirazel's guard, for such these four knights were, having waited for this occasion through all the ages of Elfland. And no more shock came to him from any of those swords, but only a vibration in his own sword's metal that passed through it like a song, and a kind of a glow that arose in it, reaching to Alveric's heart and cheering it.

But as Alveric continued to parry the swift blows of the guard, that sword that was kin to the lightning grew weary of these defences, for it had in its essence speed and desperate journeys; and, lifting Alveric's hand along with it, it swept blows at the elvish knights, and the armour of Elfland could not hold it out. Thick and curious blood began to pour through rifts in the armour, and soon of that glittering company two were fallen; and Alveric, encouraged by the zeal of his sword fought cheerily and soon overthrew another, so that only he and one of the guard remained, who seemed to have some stronger magic about him than had been given to his fallen comrades. And so it was, for when the Elf King had first enchanted the guard he had charmed this elvish soldier first of all, while all the wonder of his runes were new; and the soldier and his armour and his sword had something still of this early magic about them, more potent than any inspirations of wizardry that had come later from his master's mind. Yet this knight, as Alveric soon was able to feel along his arm and his sword, had none of those three master runes of which the old witch had spoken when she made the sword on her hill; for these were preserved unuttered by the King of Elfland himself, with which to hedge his own presence. To have known of their existence she must have flown by broom to Elfland and spoken secretly alone with the King.

And the sword that had visited Earth from so far away smote like the falling of thunderbolts; and green sparks rose from the armour, and crimson as sword met sword; and thick elvish blood moved slowly, from wide slits, down the cuirass; and Lirazel gazed in awe and wonder and love; and the combatants edged away fighting into the forest; and branches fell on them hacked off by their fight; and the runes in Alveric's far-travelled sword exulted, and roared at the elf-knight; until in the dark of the wood, amongst branches severed from disenchanted trees, with a blow like that of a thunderbolt riving an oak tree, Alveric slew him.

At that crash, and at that silence, Lirazel ran to his side.

"Quick!" she said. "For my father has three runes ..." She durst not speak of them.

"Whither?" said Alveric.

And she said: "To the fields you know."

Chapter IV

Alveric Comes Back to Earth After Many Years

Back through the guarding wood went Alveric and Lirazel, she only looking once more at those flowers and lawns, seen only by the furthest-travelling fancies of poets in deepest sleep, then urging Alveric on; he choosing the way past trees he had disenchanted.

And she would not let him delay even to choose his path, but kept urging him away from the palace that is only told of in song. And the other trees began to come lumbering towards them, from beyond the lustreless unromantic line that Alveric's sword had smitten, looking queerly as they came at their stricken comrades, whose listless branches drooped without magic or mystery. And as the moving trees came nearer Lirazel would hold up her hand, and they all halted and came on no more; and still she urged upon Alveric to hasten.

She knew her father would climb the brazen stairs of one of those silver spires, she knew he would soon come out on to a high balcony, she knew what rune he would chant. She heard the sound of his footsteps ascending, ringing now through the wood. They fled over the plain beyond the wood, all through the blue everlasting elfin day, and again and again she looked over her shoulder and urged Alveric on. The Elf King's feet boomed slow on the thousand brazen steps, and she hoped to reach the barrier of twilight, which on that side was smoky and dull; when suddenly, as she looked for the hundredth time at the distant balconies of the glittering spires, she saw a door begin to open high up, above the palace only told of in song. She cried "Alas!" to Alveric, but at that moment the scent of briar roses came drifting to them from the fields we know.

Alveric knew not fatigue for he was young, nor she for she was ageless. They rushed forward, he taking her hand; the Elf King lifted his beard, and just as he began to intone a rune that only once may be uttered, against which nothing from our fields can avail, they were through the frontier of twilight, and the rune shook and troubled those lands in which Lirazel walked no longer.

When Lirazel looked upon the fields we know, as strange to her as once they have been to us, their beauty delighted her. She laughed to see the haystacks and loved their quaintness. A lark was singing and Lirazel spoke to it, and the lark seemed not to understand, but she turned to other glories of our fields, for all were new to her, and forgot the lark. It was curiously no longer the season of bluebells, for all the foxgloves were blooming and the may was gone and the wild roses were there. Alveric never understood this.

It was early morning and the sun was shining, giving soft colours to our fields, and Lirazel rejoiced in those fields of ours at more common things than one might believe there were amongst the familiar sights of Earth's every day. So glad was she, so gay, with her cries of surprise and her laughter, that there seemed thenceforth to Alveric a beauty that he had never dreamed of in buttercups, and a humour in carts that he never had thought of before. Each moment she found with a cry of joyous discovery some treasure of Earth's that he had not known to be fair. And then, as he watched her bringing a beauty to our fields more delicate even than that the wild roses brought, he saw that her crown of ice had melted away.

And thus she came from the palace that may only be told of in song, over the fields of which I need not tell, for they were the familiar fields of Earth, that the ages change but little and only for a while, and came at evening with Alveric to his home.

All was changed in the Castle of Erl. In the gateway they met a guardian whom Alveric knew: the man wondered to see them. In the hall and upon the stairway they met some that tended the castle, who turned their heads in surprise. Alveric knew them also, but all were older; and he saw that quite ten years must have passed away during that one blue day he had spent in Elfland.

Who does not know that this is the way of Elfland? And yet who would not be surprised if they saw it happen as Alveric saw it now? He turned to Lirazel and told her how ten or twelve years were gone. But it was as though a humble man who had wed an earthly princess should tell her he had lost sixpence; time had had no value or meaning to Lirazel, and she was untroubled to hear of the ten lost years. She did not dream what time means to us here.

They told Alveric that his father was long since dead. And one told him how he died happy, without impatience, trusting to Alveric to accomplish his bidding; for he had known somewhat of the ways of Elfland, and knew that those that traffic twixt here and there must have something of that calm in which Elfland forever dreams.

Up the valley, ringing late, they heard the blacksmith's work. This blacksmith was he who had been the spokesman of those who went once to the long red room to the Lord of Erl. And all these men yet lived; for time though it moved over the Vale of Erl, as over all fields we know, moved gently, not as in our cities.

Thence Alveric and Lirazel went to the holy place of the Freer. And when they found him Alveric asked the Freer to wed them with Christom rites. And when the Freer saw the beauty of Lirazel flash mid the common things in his little holy place, for he had ornamented the walls of his house with knick-knacks that he sometimes bought at the fairs, he feared at once she was of no mortal line. And, when he asked her whence she came and she happily answered "Elfland," the good man clasped his hands and told her earnestly how all in that land dwelt beyond salvation. But she smiled, for while in Elfland she had always been idly happy, and now she only cared for Alveric. The Freer went then to his books to see what should be done.

For a long while he read in silence but for his breathing, while Alveric and Lirazel stood before him. And at last he found in his book a form of service for the wedding of a mermaid that had forsaken the sea, though the good book told not of Elfland. And this he said would suffice, for that the mermaids dwelt equally with the elf-folk beyond thought of salvation. So he sent for his bell and such tapers as are necessary. Then, turning to Lirazel, he bade her forsake and forswear and solemnly to renounce all things pertaining to Elfland, reading slowly out of a book the words to be used on this wholesome occasion.

"Good Freer," Lirazel answered, "nought said in these fields can cross the barrier of Elfland. And well that this is so, for my father has three runes that could blast this book when he answered one of its spells, were any word able to pass through the frontier of twilight. I will spell no spells with my father."

"But I cannot wed Christom man," the Freer replied, "with one of the stubborn who dwell beyond salvation."

Then Alveric implored her and she said the say in the book, "though my father could blast this spell," she added, "if it ever crossed one of his runes." And, the bell being now brought and the tapers, the good man wedded them in his little house with the rites that are proper for the wedding of a mermaid that hath forsaken the sea.

Chapter V

The Wisdom of the Parliament of Erl

In those bridal days the men of Erl came often to the castle, bringing gifts and felicitations; and in the evenings they would talk in their houses of the fair things that they hoped for the Vale of Erl on account of the wisdom of the thing they had done when they spoke with the old lord in his long red room.

There was Narl the blacksmith, who had been their leader; there was Guhic, who first had thought of it, after speaking with his wife, an upland farmer of clover pastures near Erl; there was Nehic a driver of horses; there were four vendors of beeves; and Oth, a hunter of deer; and Vlel the master-ploughman: all these and three men more had gone to the Lord of Erl and made that request that had set Alveric on his wanderings. And now they spoke of all the good that would come of it. They had all desired that the Vale of Erl should be known among men, as was, they felt, its desert. They had looked in histories, they had read books treating of pasture, yet seldom found mention at all of the vale they loved. And one day Guhic had said "Let all us people be ruled in the future by a magic lord, and he shall make the name of the valley famous, and there shall be none that have heard not the name of Erl."

And all had rejoiced and had made a parliament; and it had gone, twelve men, to the Lord of Erl. And it had been as I have told.

So now they spoke over their mead of the future of Erl, and its place among other valleys, and of the reputation that it should have in the world. They would meet and talk in the great forge of Narl, and Narl would bring them mead from an inner room, and Threl would come in late from his work in the woods. The mead was of clover honey, heavy and sweet; and when they had sat awhile in the warm room, talking of daily things of the valley and uplands, they would turn their minds to the future, seeing as through a golden mist the glory of Erl. One praised the beeves, another the horses, another the good soil, and all looked to the time when other lands should know the great mastery among valleys that was held by the valley of Erl.

And Time that brought these evenings bore them away, moving over the Vale of Erl as over all fields we know, and it was Spring again and the season of bluebells. And one day in the prime of the wild anemones, it was told that Alveric and Lirazel had a son.

Then all the people of Erl lit a fire next night on the hill, and danced about it and drank mead and rejoiced. All day they had dragged logs and branches for it from a wild wood near, and the glow of the fire was seen in other lands. Only on the pale-blue peaks of the mountains of Elfland no gleam of it shone, for they are unchanged by ought that can happen here.

And when they rested from dancing round their fires they would sit on the ground and foretell the fortune of Erl, when it should be ruled over by this son of Alveric with all the magic he would have from his mother. And some said he would lead them to war, and some said to deeper ploughing; and all foretold a better price for their beeves. None slept that night for dancing and foretelling a glorious future, and for rejoicing at the things they foretold. And above all they rejoiced that the name of Erl should be thenceforth known and honoured in other lands.

Then Alveric sought for a nurse for his child, all through the valley and uplands, and not easily found any worthy of having the care of one that was of the royal line of Elfland; and those that he found were frightened of the light, as though not of our Earth or sky, that seemed to shine at times in the baby's eyes. And in the end he went one windy morning up the hill of the lonely witch, and found her sitting idly in her doorway, having nothing to curse or bless.

"Well," said the witch, "did the sword bring you fortune?"

"Who knows," said Alveric, "what brings fortune, since we cannot see the end?"

And he spoke wearily, for he was weary with age, and never knew how many years had gone over him on the day he travelled to Elfland; far more it seemed than had passed on that same day over Erl.

"Aye," said the witch. "Who knows the end but we?"

"Mother Witch," said Alveric, "I wedded the King of Elfland's daughter."

"That was a great advancement," said the old witch.

"Mother Witch," said Alveric, "we have a child. And who shall care for him?"

"No human task," said the witch.

"Mother Witch," said Alveric, "will you come to the Vale of Erl and care for him and be the nurse at the castle? For none but you in all these fields knows ought of the things of Elfland, except the princess, and she knows nothing of Earth."

And the old witch answered: "For the sake of the King I will come."

So the witch came down from the hill with a bundle of queer belongings. And thus the child was nursed in the fields we know by one who knew songs and tales of his mother's country.

And often, as they bent together over the baby, that aged witch and the Princess Lirazel would talk together, and afterwards through long evenings, of things about which Alveric knew nothing: and for all the age of the witch, and the wisdom that she had stored in her hundred years, which is all hidden from man, it was nevertheless she who learned when they talked together, and the Princess Lirazel who taught. But of Earth and the ways of Earth Lirazel never knew anything.

And this old witch that watched over the baby so tended him and so soothed, that in all his infancy he never wept. For she had a charm for brightening the morning, and a charm for cheering the day, and a charm for calming a cough, and a charm for making the nursery warm and pleasant and eerie, when the fire leaped up at the sound of it, from logs that she had enchanted, and sent large shadows of the things about the fire quivering dark and merry over the ceiling.

And the child was cared for by Lirazel and the witch as children are cared for whose mothers are merely human; but he knew tunes and runes besides, that other children hear not in fields we know.

So the old witch moved about the nursery with her black stick, guarding the child with her runes. If a draught on windy nights shrilled in through some crack she had a spell to calm it; and a spell to charm the song that the kettle sang, till its melody brought hints of strange news from mist-hidden places, and the child grew to know the mystery of far valleys that his eyes had never seen. And at evening she would raise her ebon stick and, standing before the fire amongst all the shadows, would enchant them and make them dance for him. And they took all manner of shapes of good and evil, dancing to please the baby; so that he came to have knowledge not only of the things with which Earth is stored; pigs, trees, camels, crocodiles, wolves, and ducks, good dogs and the gentle cow; but of the darker things also that men have feared, and the things they have hoped and guessed. Through those evenings the things that happen, and the creatures that are, passed over those nursery walls, and he grew familiar with the fields we know. And on warm afternoons the witch would carry him through the village, and all the dogs would bark at her eerie figure, but durst not come too close, for a page-boy behind her carried the ebon stick. And dogs, that know so much, that know how far a man can throw a stone, and if he would beat them, and if he durst not, knew also that this was no ordinary stick. So they kept far away from that queer black stick in the hand of the page, and snarled, and the villagers came out to see. And all were glad when they saw how magical a nurse the young heir had, "for here," they said, "is the witch Ziroonderel," and they declared that she would bring him up amongst the true principles of wizardry, and that in his time there would be magic that would make all their valley famous. And they beat their dogs until they slunk indoors, but the dogs clung to their suspicions still. So that when the men were gone to the forge of Narl, and their houses were quiet in the moonlight and Narl's windows glowed, and the mead had gone round, and they talked of the future of Erl, more and more voices joining in the tale of its coming glory, on soft feet the dogs would come out to the sandy street and howl.

And to the high sunny nursery Lirazel would come, bringing a brightness that the learned witch had not in all her spells, and would sing to her boy those songs that none can sing to us here, for they were learned the other side of the frontier of twilight and were made by singers all unvexed by Time. And for all the marvel that there was in those songs, whose origin was so far from the fields we know, and in times remote from those that historians use; and though men wondered at the strangeness of them when from open casements through the Summer days they drifted over Erl; yet none wondered even at those as she wondered at the earthly ways of her child and all the little human things that he did more and more as he grew. For all human ways were strange to her. And yet she loved him more than her father's realm, or the glittering centuries of her ageless youth, or the palace that may be told of only in song.

In those days Alveric learned that she would never now grow familiar with earthly things, never understand the folk that dwelt in the valley, never read wise books without laughter, never care for earthly ways, never feel more at ease in the Castle of Erl than any woodland thing that Threl might have snared and kept caged in a house. He had hoped that soon she would learn the things that were strange to her, till the little differences that there are between things in our fields and in Elfland should not trouble her any more; but he saw at last that the things that were strange would always so remain, and that all the centuries of her timeless home had not so lightly shaped her thoughts and fancies that they could be altered by our brief years here. When he had learned this he had learned the truth.

Between the spirits of Alveric and Lirazel lay all the distance there is between Earth and Elfland; and love bridged the distance, which can bridge further than that; yet when for a moment on the golden bridge he would pause and let his thoughts look down at the gulf, all his mind would grow giddy and Alveric trembled. What of the end, he thought? And feared lest it should be stranger than the beginning.

And she, she did not see that she should know anything. Was not her beauty enough? Had not a lover come at last to those lawns that shone by the palace only told of in song, and rescued her from her uncompanioned fate and from that perpetual calm? Was it not enough that he had come? Must she needs understand the curious things folk did? Must she never dance in the road, never speak to goats, never laugh at funerals, never sing at night? Why! What was joy for if it must be hidden? Must merriment bow to dulness in these strange fields she had come to? And then one day she saw how a woman of Erl looked less fair than she had looked a year ago. Little enough was the change, but her swift eye saw it surely. And she went to Alveric crying to be comforted, because she feared that Time in the fields we know might have power to harm that beauty that the long long ages of Elfland had never dared to dim. And Alveric had said that Time must have his way, as all men know; and where was the good of complaining?

Chapter VI

The Rune of the Elf King

On the high balcony of his gleaming tower the King of Elfland stood. Below him echoed yet the thousand steps. He had lifted his head to chant the rune that should hold his daughter in Elfland, and in that moment had seen her pass the murky barrier; which on this side, facing toward Elfland, is all lustrous with twilight, and on that side, facing towards the fields we know, is smoky and angry and dull. And now he had dropped his head till his beard lay mingled with his cape of ermine above his cerulean cloak, and stood there silently sorrowful, while time passed swift as ever over the fields we know.

And standing there all blue and white against his silver tower, aged by the passing of times of which we know nothing, before he imposed its eternal calm upon Elfland, he thought of his daughter amongst our pitiless years. For he knew, whose wisdom surpassed the confines of Elfland and touched our rugged fields, knew well the harshness of material things and all the turmoil of Time. Even as he stood there he knew that the years that assail beauty, and the myriad harshnesses that vex the spirit, were already about his daughter. And the days that remained to her now seemed scarce more to him, dwelling beyond the fret and ruin of Time, than to us might seem a briar rose's hours when plucked and foolishly hawked in the streets of a city. He knew that there hung over her now the doom of all mortal things. He thought of her perishing soon, as mortal things must; to be buried amongst the rocks of a land that scorned Elfland and that held its most treasured myths to be of little account. And were he not the King of all that magical land, which held its eternal calm from his own mysterious serenity, he had wept to think of the grave in rocky Earth gripping that form that was so fair forever. Or else, he thought, she would pass to some paradise far from his knowledge, some heaven of which books told in the fields we know, for he had heard even of this. He pictured her on some apple-haunted hill, under blossoms of an everlasting April, through which flickered the pale gold haloes of those that had cursed Elfland. He saw, though dimly for all his magical wisdom, the glory that only the blessed clearly see. He saw his daughter on those heavenly hills stretch out both arms, as he knew well she would, towards the pale-blue peaks of her elfin home, while never one of the blessed heeded her yearning. And then, though he was king of all that land, that had its everlasting calm from him, he wept and all Elfland shivered. It shivered as placid water shivers here if something suddenly touches it from our fields.

Then the King turned and left his balcony and went in great haste down his brazen steps.

He came clanging to the ivory doors that shut the tower below, and through them came to the throne-room of which only song may tell. And there he took a parchment out of a coffer and a plume from some fabulous wing, and dipping the plume into no earthly ink, wrote out a rune on the parchment. Then raising two fingers he made the minor enchantment whereby he summoned his guard. And no guard came.

I have said that no time passed at all in Elfland. Yet the happening of events is in itself a manifestation of time, and no event can occur unless time pass. Now it is thus with time in Elfland: in the eternal beauty that dreams in that honied air nothing stirs or fades or dies, nothing seeks its happiness in movement or change or a new thing, but has its ecstasy in the perpetual contemplation of all the beauty that has ever been, and which always glows over those enchanted lawns as intense as when first created by incantation or song. Yet if the energies of the wizard's mind arose to meet a new thing, then that power that had laid its calm upon Elfland and held back time troubled the calm awhile, and time for awhile shook Elfland. Cast anything into a deep pool from a land strange to it, where some great fish dreams, and green weeds dream, and heavy colours dream, and light sleeps; the great fish stirs, the colours shift and change, the green weeds tremble, the light wakes, a myriad things know slow movement and change; and soon the whole pool is still again. It was the same when Alveric passed through the border of twilight and right through the enchanted wood, and the King was troubled and moved, and all Elfland trembled.

When the King saw that no guard came he looked into the wood which he knew to be troubled, through the deep mass of the trees, that were quivering yet with the coming of Alveric; he looked through the deeps of the wood and the silver walls of his palace, for he looked by enchantment, and there he saw the four knights of his guard lying stricken upon the ground with their thick elvish blood hanging out through slits in their armour. And he thought of the early magic whereby he had made the eldest, with a rune all newly inspired, before he had conquered Time. He passed out through the splendour and glow of one of his flashing portals, and over a gleaming lawn and came to the fallen guard, and saw the trees still troubled.

"There has been magic here," said the King of Elfland.

And then though he only had three runes that could do such a thing, and though they only could be uttered once, and one was already written upon parchment to bring his daughter home, he uttered the second of his most magical runes over that elder knight that his magic had made long ago. And in the silence that followed the last words of the rune the rents in the moon-bright armour all clicked shut at once, and the thick dark blood was gone and the knight rose live to his feet. And the Elf King now had only one rune left that was mightier than any magic we know.

The other three knights lay dead; and, having no souls, their magic returned again to the mind of their master.

He went back then to his palace, while he sent the last of his guard to fetch him a troll.

Dark brown of skin and two or three feet high the trolls are a gnomish tribe that inhabit Elfland. And soon there was a scamper in the throne-room that may only be told of in song, and a troll lit by the throne on its two bare feet and stood before its king. The King gave it the parchment with the rune written thereon, saying: "Scamper hence, and pass over the end of the Land, until you come to the fields that none know here; and find the Princess Lirazel who is gone to the haunts of men, and give her this rune and she shall read it and all shall be well."

And the troll scampered thence.

And soon the troll was come with long leaps to the frontier of twilight. Then nothing moved in Elfland any more; and motionless on that splendid throne of which only song may speak sat the old King mourning in silence.

Chapter VII

The Coming of the Troll

When the troll came to the frontier of twilight he skipped nimbly through; yet he emerged cautiously into the fields we know, for he was afraid of dogs. Slipping quietly out of those dense masses of twilight he came so softly into our fields that no eye had seen him unless it were gazing already at the spot at which he appeared. There he paused for some instants, looking to left and right; and, seeing no dogs, he left the barrier of twilight. This troll had never before been in the fields we know, yet he knew well to avoid dogs, for the fear of dogs is so deep and universal amongst all that are less than Man, that it seems to have passed even beyond our boundaries and to have been felt in Elfland.

In our fields it was now May, and the buttercups stretched away before the troll, a world of yellow mingled with the brown of the budding grasses. When he saw so many buttercups shining there the wealth of Earth astonished him. And soon he was moving through them, yellowing his shins as he went.

He had not gone far from Elfland when he met with a hare, who was lying in a comfortable arrangement of grass, in which he had intended to pass the time till he should have things to see to.

When the hare saw the troll he sat there without any movement whatever, and without any expression in his eyes, and did nothing at all but think.

When the troll saw the hare he skipped nearer, and lay down before it in the buttercups, and asked it the way to the haunts of men. And the hare went on thinking.

"Thing of these fields," repeated the troll, "where are the haunts of men?"

The hare got up then and walked towards the troll, which made the hare look very ridiculous, for he had none of the grace while walking that he has when he runs or gambols, and was much lower in front than behind. He put his nose into the troll's face and twitched foolish whiskers.

"Tell me the way," said the troll.

When the hare perceived that the troll did not smell of anything like dog he was content to let the troll question him. But he did not understand the language of Elfland, so he lay still again and thought while the troll talked.

And at last the troll wearied of getting no answer, so he leaped up and shouted "Dogs!" and left the hare and scampered away merrily over the buttercups, taking any direction that led away from Elfland. And though the hare could not quite understand elvish language, yet there was a vehemence in the tone in which the troll had shouted Dogs which caused apprehension to enter the thoughts of the hare, so that very soon he forsook his arrangement of grass, and lollopped away through the meadow with one scornful look after the troll; but he did not go very fast, going mostly on three legs, with one hind leg all ready to let down if there should really be dogs. And soon he paused and sat up and put up his ears, and looked across the buttercups and thought deeply. And before the hare had ceased to ponder the troll's meaning the troll was far out of sight and had forgotten what he had said.

And soon he saw the gables of a farm-house rise up beyond a hedge. They seemed to look at him with little windows up under red tiles. "A haunt of man," said the troll. And yet some elvish instinct seemed to tell him that it was not here that Princess Lirazel had come. Still, he went nearer the farm and began to gaze at its poultry. But just at that moment a dog saw him, one that had never seen a troll before, and it uttered one canine cry of astonished indignation, and keeping all the rest of its breath for the chase, sped after the troll.

The troll began at once to rise and dip over the buttercups as though he had almost borrowed its speed from the swallow and were riding the lower air. Such speed was new to the dog, and he went in a long curve after the troll, leaning over as he went, his mouth open and silent, the wind rippling all the way from his nose to his tail in one wavy current. The curve was made by the dog's baffled hopes to catch the troll as he slanted across. Soon he was straight behind; and the troll toyed with speed; breathing the flowery air in long fresh draughts above the tops of the buttercups. He thought no more of the dog, but he did not cease in the flight that the dog had caused, because of the joy of the speed. And this strange chase continued over those fields, the troll driven on by joy and the dog by duty. For the sake of novelty then the troll put his feet together as he leaped over the flowers and, alighting with rigid knees, fell forwards on to his hands and so turned over; and, straightening his elbows suddenly as he turned, shot himself into the air still turning over and over. He did this several times, increasing the indignation of the dog, who knew well enough that that was no way to go over the fields we know. But for all his indignation the dog had seen clear enough that he would never catch that troll, and presently he returned to the farm, and found his master there and went up to him wagging his tail. So hard he wagged it that the farmer was sure he had done some useful thing, and patted him, and there the matter ended.

And it was well enough for the farmer that his dog has chased that troll from his farm; for had it communicated to his livestock any of the wonder of Elfland they would have mocked at Man, and that farmer would have lost the allegiance of all but his staunch dog.

And the troll went on gaily over the tips of the buttercups.

Presently he saw rising up all white over the flowers a fox that was facing him with his white chest and chin, and watching the troll as it went. The troll went near to him and took a look. And the fox went on watching him, for the fox watches all things.

He had come back lately to those dewy fields from slinking by night along the boundary of twilight that lies between here and Elfland. He even prowls inside the very boundary, walking amongst the twilight; and it is in the mystery of that heavy twilight that lies between here and there that there clings to him some of that glamour that he brings with him to our fields.

"Well, Noman's Dog," said the troll. For they know the fox in Elfland, from seeing him often go dimly along their borders; and this is the name they give him.

"Well, Thing-over-the-Border," said the fox when he answered at all. For he knew troll-talk.

"Are the haunts of men near here?" said the troll.

The fox moved his whiskers by slightly wrinkling his lip. Like all liars he reflected before he spoke, and sometimes even let wise silences do better than speech.

"Men live here and men live there," said the fox.

"I want their haunts," said the troll.

"What for?" said the fox.

"I have a message from the King of Elfland."

The fox showed no respect or fear at the mention of that dread name, but slightly moved his head and eyes to conceal the awe that he felt.

"If it is a message," he said, "their haunts are over there." And he pointed with his long thin nose towards Erl.

"How shall I know when I get there?" said the troll.

"By the smell," said the fox. "It is a big haunt of men, and the smell is dreadful."

"Thanks, Noman's Dog," said the troll. And he seldom thanked anyone.

"I should never go near them," said the fox, "but for ..." And he paused and reflected silently.

"But for what?" said the troll.

"But for their poultry." And he fell into a grave silence.

"Good-bye, Noman's Dog," said the troll and turned head-over-heels, and was off on his way to Erl.

Passing over the buttercups all through the dewy morning the troll was far on his way by the afternoon, and saw before evening the smoke and the towers of Erl. It was all sunk in a hollow; and gables and chimneys and towers peered over the lip of the valley, and smoke hung over them on the dreamy air. "The haunts of men," said the troll. Then he sat down amongst the grasses and looked at it.

Presently he went nearer and looked at it again. He did not like the look of the smoke and that crowd of gables: certainly it smelt dreadfully. There had been some legend in Elfland of the wisdom of Man; and whatever respect that legend had gained for us in the light mind of the troll now all blew lightly away as he looked at the crowded houses. And as he looked at them there passed a child of four, a small girl on a footpath over the fields, going home in the evening to Erl. They looked at each other with round eyes.

"Hullo," said the child.

"Hullo, Child of Men," said the troll.

He was not speaking troll-talk now, but the language of Elfland, that grander tongue that he had had to speak when he was before the King: for he knew the language of Elfland although it was never used in the homes of the trolls, who preferred troll-talk. This language was spoken in those days also by men, for there were fewer languages then, and the elves and the people of Erl both used the same.

"What are you?" said the child.

"A troll of Elfland," answered the troll.

"So I thought," said the child.

"Where are you going, child of men?" the troll asked.

"To the houses," the child replied.

"We don't want to go there," said the troll.

"N-no," said the child.

"Come to Elfland," the troll said.

The child thought for awhile. Other children had gone, and the elves always sent a changeling in their place, so that nobody quite missed them and nobody really knew. She thought awhile of the wonder and wildness of Elfland, and then of her own home.

"N-no," said the child.

"Why not?" said the troll.

"Mother made a jam roll this morning," said the child. And she walked on gravely home. Had it not been for that chance jam roll she had gone to Elfland.

"Jam!" said the troll contemptuously and thought of the tarns of Elfland, the great lily-leaves lying flat upon their solemn waters, the huge blue lilies towering into the elf-light above the green deep tarns: for jam this child had forsaken them!

Then he thought of his duty again, the roll of parchment and the Elf King's rune for his daughter. He had carried the parchment in his left hand when he ran, in his mouth when he somersaulted over the buttercups. Was the Princess here he thought? Or were there other haunts of men? As evening drew in he crept nearer and nearer the homes, to hear without being seen.

Chapter VIII

The Arrival of the Rune

On a sunny May morning in Erl the witch Ziroonderel sat in the castle nursery by the fire, cooking a meal for the baby. The boy was now three years old, and still Lirazel had not named him; for she feared lest some jealous spirit of Earth or air should hear the name, and if so she would not say what she feared then. And Alveric had said he must be named.

And the boy could bowl a hoop; for the witch had gone one misty night to her hill and had brought him a moon-halo which she got by enchantment at moonrise, and had hammered it into a hoop, and had made him a little rod of thunderbolt-iron with which to beat it along.

And now the boy was waiting for his breakfast; and there was a spell across the threshold to keep the nursery snug, which Ziroonderel had put there with a wave of her ebon stick, and it kept out rats and mice and dogs, nor could bats sail across it, and the watchful nursery cat it kept at home: no lock that blacksmiths made was any stronger.

Suddenly over the threshold and over the spell the troll jumped somersaulting through the air and came down sitting. The crude wooden nursery-clock hanging over the fire stopped its loud tick as he came; for he bore with him a little charm against time, with strange grass round one of his fingers, that he might not be withered away in the fields we know. For well the Elf King knew the flight of our hours: four years had swept over these fields of ours while he had boomed down his brazen steps and sent for his troll and given him that spell to bind round one of his fingers.

"What's this?" said Ziroonderel.

That troll knew well when to be impudent, but looking in the witch's eyes saw something to be afraid of; and well he might, for those eyes had looked in the Elf King's own. Therefore he played, as we say in these fields, his best card, and answered: "A message from the King of Elfland."

"Is that so?" said the old witch. "Yes, yes," she added more lowly to herself, "that would be for my lady. Yes, that would come."

The troll sat still on the floor fingering the roll of parchment inside of which was written the rune of the King of Elfland. Then over the end of his bed, as he waited for breakfast, the baby saw the troll, and asked him who he was and where he came from and what he was able to do. When the baby asked him what he was able to do the troll jumped up and skipped about the room like a moth on a lamp-lit ceiling. From floor to shelves and back and up again he went with leaps like flying; the baby clapped his hands, the cat was furious; the witch raised her ebon stick and made a charm against leaping, but it could not hold the troll. He leaped and bounced and bounded, while the cat hissed all the curses that the feline language knows, and Ziroonderel was wrath not only because her magic was thwarted, but because with mere human alarm she feared for her cups and saucers; and the baby shouted all the while for more. And all at once the troll remembered his errand and the dread parchment he bore.

"Where is the Princess Lirazel?" he said to the witch.

And the witch pointed the way to the princess's tower; for she knew that there were no means nor power she had by which to hinder a rune from the King of Elfland. And as the troll turned to go Lirazel entered the room. He bowed all low before this great lady of Elfland and, with all his impudence in a moment lost, kneeled on one knee before the blaze of her beauty and presented the Elf King's rune. The boy was shouting to his mother to demand more leaps from the troll, as she took the scroll in her hand; the cat with her back to a box was watching alertly; Ziroonderel was all silent.

And then the troll thought of the weed-green tarns of Elfland in the woods that the trolls knew; he thought of the wonder of the unwithering flowers that time has never touched; the deep, deep colour and the perpetual calm: his errand was over and he was weary of Earth.

For a moment nothing moved there but the baby, shouting for new troll antics and waving his arms: Lirazel stood with the elfin scroll in her hand, the troll knelt before her, the witch never stirred, the cat stood watching fiercely, even the clock was still. Then the Princess moved and the troll rose to his feet, the witch sighed and the cat gave up her watchfulness as the troll scampered away. And though the baby shouted for the troll to return it never heeded, but twisted down the long spiral stairs, and slipping out through a door was off towards Elfland. As the troll passed over the threshold the wooden clock ticked again.

Lirazel looked at the scroll and looked at her boy, and did not unroll the parchment, but turned and carried it away, and came to her chamber and locked the scroll in a casket, and left it there unread. For her fears told her well the most potent rune of her father, that she had dreaded so much as she fled from his silver tower and heard his feet go booming up the brass, had crossed the frontier of twilight written upon the scroll, and would meet her eyes the moment she unrolled it and waft her thence.

When the rune was safe in the casket she went to Alveric to tell him of the peril that had come near her. But Alveric was troubled because she would not name the baby, and asked her at once about this. And so she suggested a name at last to him; and it was one that no one in these fields could pronounce, an elvish name full of wonder, and made of syllables like birds' cries at night. Alveric would have none of it. And her whim in this came, as all the whims she had, from no customary thing of these fields of ours, but sheer over the border from Elfland, sheer over the border with all wild fancies that rarely visit our fields. And Alveric was vexed with these whims, for there had been none like them of old in the Castle of Erl: none could interpret them to him and none advise him. He looked for her to be guided by old customs; she looked only for some wild fancy to come from the southeast. He reasoned with her with the human reason that folk set much store by here, but she did not want reason. And so when they parted she had not after all told anything of the peril that had sought her from Elfland, which she had come to Alveric to tell.

She went instead to her tower and looked at the casket, shining there in the low late light; and turned from it and often looked again; while the light went under the fields and the gloaming came, and all glimmered away. She sat then by the casement open towards eastern hills, above whose darkening curves she watched the stars. She watched so long that she saw them change their places. For more than all things else that she had seen since she came to these fields of ours she had wondered at the stars. She loved their gentle beauty; and yet she was sad as she looked wistfully to them, for Alveric had said that she must not worship them.

How if she might not worship them could she give them their due, could she thank them for their beauty, could she praise their joyful calm? And then she thought of her baby: then she saw Orion: then she defied all jealous spirits of air, and, looking toward Orion, whom she must never worship, she offered her baby's days to that belted hunter, naming her baby after those splendid stars.

And when Alveric came to the tower she told him of her wish, and he was willing the boy should be named Orion, for all in that valley set much store by hunting. And the hope came back to Alveric, which he would not put away, that being reasonable at last in this, she would now be reasonable in all other things, and be guided by custom, and do what others did, and forsake wild whims and fancies that came over the border from Elfland. And he asked her to worship the holy things of the Freer. For never had she given any of these things their due, and knew not which was the holier, his candlestick or his bell, and never would learn for ought that Alveric told her.

And now she answered him pleasantly and her husband thought all was well, but her thoughts were far with Orion; nor did they ever tarry with grave things long, nor could tarry longer amongst them than butterflies do in the shade.

All that night the casket was locked on the rune of the King of Elfland.

And next morning Lirazel gave little thought to the rune, for they went with the boy to the holy place of the Freer; and Ziroonderel came with them but waited without. And the folk of Erl came too, as many as could leave the affairs of man with the fields; and all were there of those that had made the parliament, when they went to Alveric's sire in the long red room. And all of these were glad when they saw the boy and marked his strength and growth; and, muttering low together as they stood in the holy place, they foretold how all should be as they had planned. And the Freer came forth and, standing amongst his holy things, he gave to the boy before him the name of Orion, though he sooner had given some name of those that he knew to be blessed. And he rejoiced to see the boy and to name him there; for by the family that dwelt in the Castle of Erl all these folk marked the generations, and watched the ages pass, as sometimes we watch the seasons go over some old known tree. And he bowed himself before Alveric, and was full courteous to Lirazel, yet his courtesy to the princess came not from his heart, for in his heart he held her in no more reverence than he held a mermaid that had forsaken the sea.

And the boy came even so by the name of Orion. And all the folk rejoiced as he came out with his parents and rejoined Ziroonderel at the edge of the holy garden. And Alveric, Lirazel, Ziroonderel and Orion all walked back to the castle.

And all that day Lirazel did nothing that caused anybody to wonder, but let herself be governed by custom and the ways of the fields we know. Only, when the stars came out and Orion shone, she knew that their splendour had not received its due, and her gratitude to Orion yearned to be said. She was grateful for his bright beauty that cheered our fields, and grateful for his protection, of which she felt sure for her boy, against jealous spirits of air. And all her unsaid thanks so burned in her heart that all of a sudden she rose and left her tower and went out to the open starlight, and lifted her face to the stars and the place of Orion, and stood all dumb though her thanks were trembling upon her lips; for Alveric had told her one must not pray to the stars. With face upturned to all that wandering host she stood long silent, obedient to Alveric: then she lowered her eyes, and there was a small pool glimmering in the night, in which all the faces of the stars were shining. "To pray to the stars," she said to herself in the night, "is surely wrong. These images in the water are not the stars. I will pray to their images, and the stars will know."

And on her knees amongst the iris leaves she prayed at the edge of the pool, and gave thanks to the images of the stars for the joy she had had of the night, when the constellations shone in their myriad majesty, and moved like an army dressed in silver mail, marching from unknown victories to conquer in distant wars. She blessed and thanked and praised those bright reflections shimmering down in the pool, and bade them tell her thanks and her praise to Orion, to whom she might not pray. It was thus that Alveric found her, kneeling, bent down in the dark, and reproached her bitterly. She was worshipping the stars, he said, which were there for no such purpose. And she said she was only supplicating their images.

We may understand his feelings easily: the strangeness of her, her unexpected acts, her contrariness to all established things, her scorn for custom, her wayward ignorance, jarred on some treasured tradition every day. The more romantic she had been far away over the frontier, as told of by legend and song, the more difficult it was for her to fill any place once held by the ladies of that castle who were versed in all the lore of the fields we know. And Alveric looked for her to fulfil duties and follow customs which were all as new to her as the twinkling stars.

But Lirazel felt only that the stars had not their due, and that custom or reason or whatever men set store by should demand that thanks be given them for their beauty; and she had not thanked them even, but had supplicated only their images in the pool.

That night she thought of Elfland, where all things were matched with her beauty, where nothing changed and there were no strange customs, and no strange magnificences like these stars of ours to whom none gave their due. She thought of the elfin lawns and the towering banks of the flowers, and the palace that may not be told of but only in song.

Still locked in the dark of the casket the rune bided its time.

Chapter IX

Lirazel Blows Away

And the days went by, the Summer passed over Erl, the sun that had travelled northward fared South again, it was near to the time when the swallows left those eaves, and Lirazel had not learnt anything. She had not prayed to the stars again, or supplicated their images, but she had learned no human customs, and could not see why her love and gratitude must remain unexpressed to the stars. And Alveric did not know that the time must come when some simple trivial thing would divide them utterly.

And then one day, hoping still, he took her with him to the house of the Freer to teach her how to worship his holy things. And gladly the good man brought his candle and bell, and the eagle of brass that held up his book when he read, and a little symbolic bowl that had scented water, and the silver snuffers that put his candle out. And he told her clearly and simply, as he had told her before, the origin, meaning and mystery of all these things, and why the bowl was of brass and the snuffer of silver, and what the symbols were that were carved on the bowl. With fitting courtesy he told her these things, even with kindness; and yet there was something in his voice as he told, a little distant from her; and she knew that he spoke as one that walked safe on shore calling far to a mermaid amid dangerous seas.

As they came back to the castle the swallows were grouped to go, sitting in lines along the battlements. And Lirazel had promised to worship the holy things of the Freer, like the simple bell-fearing folk of the valley of Erl: and a late hope was shining in Alveric's mind that even yet all was well. And for many days she remembered all that the Freer had told her.

And one day walking late from the nursery, past tall windows to her tower, and looking out on the evening, remembering that she must not worship the stars, she called to mind the holy things of the Freer, and tried to remember all she was told of them. It seemed so hard to worship them just as she should. She knew that before many hours the swallows would all be gone; and often when they left her her mood would change; and she feared that she might forget, and never remember more, how she ought to worship the holy things of the Freer.

So she went out into the night again over the grasses to where a thin brook ran, and drew out some great flat pebbles that she knew where to find, turning her face away from the images of the stars. By day the stones shone beautifully in the water, all ruddy and mauve; now they were all dark. She drew them out and laid them in the meadow: she loved these smooth flat stones, for somehow they made her remember the rocks of Elfland.

She laid them all in a row, this for the candlestick, this for the bell, that for the holy bowl. "If I can worship these lovely stones as things ought to be worshipped," she said, "I can worship the things of the Freer."

Then she kneeled down before the big flat stones and prayed to them as though they were Christom things.

And Alveric seeking her in the wide night, wondering what wild fancy had carried her whither, heard her voice in the meadow, crooning such prayers as are offered to holy things.

When he saw the four flat stones to which she prayed, bowed down before them in the grass, he said that no worse than this were the darkest ways of the heathen. And she said "I am learning to worship the holy things of the Freer."

"It is the art of the heathen," he said.

Now of all things that men feared in the valley of Erl they feared most the arts of the heathen, of whom they knew nothing but that their ways were dark. And he spoke with the anger which men always used when they spoke there of the heathen. And his anger went to her heart, for she was but learning to worship his holy things to please him, and yet he had spoken like this.

And Alveric would not speak the words that should have been said, to turn aside anger and soothe her; for no man, he foolishly thought, should compromise in matters touching on heathenesse. So Lirazel went alone all sadly back to her tower. And Alveric stayed to cast the four flat stones afar.

And the swallows left, and unhappy days went by. And one day Alveric bade her worship the holy things of the Freer, and she had quite forgotten how. And he spoke again of the arts of heathenesse. The day was shining and the poplars golden and all the aspens red.

Then Lirazel went to her tower and opened the casket, that shone in the morning with the clear autumnal light, and took in her hand the rune of the King of Elfland, and carried it with her across the high vaulted hall, and came to another tower and climbed its steps to the nursery.

And there all day she stayed and played with her child, with the scroll still tight in her hand: and, merrily though she played at whiles, yet there were strange calms in her eyes, which Ziroonderel watched while she wondered. And when the sun was low and she had put the child to bed she sat beside him all solemn as she told him childish tales. And Ziroonderel, the wise witch, watched; and for all her wisdom only guessed how it would be, and knew not how to make it otherwise.

And before sunset Lirazel kissed the boy and unrolled the Elf King's scroll. It was but a petulance that had made her take it from the coffer in which it lay, and the petulance might have passed and she might not have unrolled the scroll, only that it was there in her hand. Partly petulance, partly wonder, partly whims too idle to name, drew her eyes to the Elf King's words in their coal-black curious characters.

And whatever magic there was in the rune of which I cannot tell (and dreadful magic there was), the rune was written with love that was stronger than magic, till those mystical characters glowed with the love that the Elf King had for his daughter, and there were blended in that mighty rune two powers, magic and love, the greatest power there is beyond the boundary of twilight with the greatest power there is in the fields we know. And if Alveric's love could have held her he should have trusted alone to that love, for the Elf King's rune was mightier than the holy things of the Freer.

No sooner had Lirazel read the rune on the scroll than fancies from Elfland began to pour over the border. Some came that would make a clerk in the City to-day leave his desk at once to dance on the sea-shore; and some would have driven all the men in a bank to leave doors and coffers open and wander away till they came to green open land and the heathery hills; and some would have made a poet of a man, all of a sudden as he sat at his business. They were mighty fancies that the Elf King summoned by the force of his magical rune. And Lirazel sat there with the rune in her hand, helpless amongst this mass of tumultuous fancies from Elfland. And as the fancies raged and sang and called, more and more over the border, all crowding on one poor mind, her body grew lighter and lighter. Her feet half rested half floated, upon the floor; Earth scarcely held her down, so fast was she becoming a thing of dreams. No love of hers for Earth, or of the children of Earth for her, had any longer power to hold her there.

And now came memories of her ageless childhood beside the tarns of Elfland, by the deep forest's border, by those delirious lawns, or in the palace that may not be told of except only in song. She saw those things as clearly as we see small shells in water, looking through clear ice down to the floor of some sleeping lake, a little dimmed in that other region across the barrier of ice; so too her memories shone a little dimly from across the frontier of Elfland. Little queer sounds of elfin creatures came to her, scents swam from those miraculous flowers that glowed by the lawns she knew, faint sounds of enchanted songs blew over the border and reached her seated there, voices and melodies and memories came floating through the twilight, all Elfland was calling. Then measured and resonant, and strangely near, she heard her father's voice.

She rose at once, and now Earth had lost on her the grip that it only has on material things, and a thing of dreams and fancy and fable and phantasy she drifted from the room; and Ziroonderel had no power to hold her with any spell, nor had she herself the power even to turn, even to look at her boy as she drifted away.

And at that moment a wind came out of the north-west, and entered the woods and bared the golden branches, and danced on over the downs, and led a company of scarlet and golden leaves, that had dreaded this day but danced now it had come; and away with a riot of dancing and glory of colour, high in the light of the sun that had set from the sight of the fields, went wind and leaves together. With them went Lirazel.

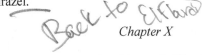

Back to Elfland

Chapter X

The Ebbing of Elfland

Next morning Alveric came up the tower to the witch Ziroonderel, weary and frantic from searching all night long in strange places for Lirazel. All night he had tried to guess what fancy had beckoned her out and whither it might have led her; he had searched by the stream by which she had prayed to the stones, and the pool where she prayed to the stars; he had called her name up every tower, and had called it wide in the dark, and had had no answer but echo; and so he had come at last to the witch Ziroonderel.

"Whither?" he said, saying no more than that, that the boy might not know his fears. Yet Orion knew.

And Ziroonderel all mournfully shook her head. "The way of the leaves," she said. "The way of all beauty."

But Alveric did not stay to hear her say more than her first five words; for he went with the restlessness with which he had come, straight from the room and hastily down the stair, and out at once into the windy morning, to see which way those glorious leaves were gone.

And a few leaves that had clung to cold branches longer, when the gay company of their comrades had gone, were now too on the air, going lonely and last: and Alveric saw they were going south-east towards Elfland.

Hurriedly then he donned his magical sword in its wide scabbard of leather; and with scanty provisions hastened over the fields, after the last of the leaves, whose autumnal glory led him, as many a cause in its latter days, all splendid and fallen, leads all manner of men.

And so he came to the upland fields with their grass all grey with dew; and the air was all sparkling with sunlight, and gay with the last of the leaves, but a melancholy seemed to dwell with the sound of the lowing of cattle.

In the calm bright morning with the north-west wind roaming through it Alveric came by no calm, and never gave up the haste of one who has lost something suddenly: he had the swift movements of such, and the frantic air. He watched all day over clear wide horizons, south-east where the leaves were leading; and at evening he looked to see the

Elfin Mountains, severe and changeless, unlit by any light we know, the colour of pale forget-me-nots. He held on restlessly to see their summits, but never they came to view.

And then he saw the house of the old leather-worker who had made the scabbard for his sword; and the sight of it brought back to him the years that were gone since the evening when first he had seen it, although he never knew how many they were, and could not know, for no one has ever devised any exact calculation whereby to estimate the action of time in Elfland. Then he looked once more for the pale-blue Elfin Mountains, remembering well where they lay, in their long grave row past a point of one of the leather-worker's gables, but he saw never a line of them. Then he entered the house and the old man still was there.

The leather-worker was wonderfully aged; even the table on which he worked was much older. He greeted Alveric, remembering who he was, and Alveric enquired for the old man's wife. "She died long ago," he said. And again Alveric felt the baffling flight of those years, which added a fear to Elfland whither he went, yet he neither thought to turn back nor reined for a moment his impatient haste. He said a few formal things of the old man's loss that had happened so long ago. Then "Where are the Elfin Mountains," he asked, "the pale-blue peaks?"

A look came slowly over the old man's face as though he had never seen them, as though Alveric being learned spoke of something that the old leather-worker could not know. No, he did not know, he said. And Alveric found that to-day as all those years ago, this old man still refused to speak of Elfland. Well, the boundary was only a few yards away; he would cross it and ask the way of elfin creatures, if he could not see the mountains to guide him then. The old man offered him food, and he had not eaten all day; but Alveric in his haste only asked him once more of Elfland, and the old man humbly said that of such things he knew nothing. Then Alveric strode away and came to the field he knew, which he remembered to be divided by the nebulous border of twilight. And indeed he had no sooner come to the field than he saw all the toadstools leaning over one way, and that the way he was going; for just as thorn trees all lean away from the sea, so toadstools and every plant that has any touch of mystery, such as foxgloves, mulleins and certain kinds of orchis, when growing anywhere near it, all lean towards Elfland. By this one may know before one has heard a murmur of waves, or before one has guessed an influence of magical things, that one comes, as the case may be, to the sea or the border of Elfland. And in the air above him Alveric saw golden birds, and guessed that there had been a storm in Elfland blowing them over the border from the south-east, though a north-west wind blew over the fields we know. And he went on but the boundary was not there, and he crossed the field as any field we know, and still he had not come to the fells of Elfland.

Then Alveric pressed on with a new impatience, with the north-west wind behind him. And the Earth began to grow bare and shingly and dull, without flowers, without shade, without colour, with none of those things that there are in remembered lands, by which we build pictures of them when we are there no more; it was all disenchanted now. Alveric saw a golden bird high up, rushing away to the south-east; and he followed his flight hoping soon to see the mountains of Elfland, which he supposed to be merely concealed by some magical mist.

But still the autumnal sky was bright and clear, and all the horizon plain, and still there came never a gleam of the Elfin Mountains. And not from this did he learn that Elfland had ebbed. But when he saw on that desolate shingly plain, untorn by the north-west wind but blooming fair in the Autumn, a may tree that he remembered a long while since, all white with blossom that once rejoiced a Spring day far in his childhood, then he knew that Elfland had been there and must have receded, although he knew not how far. For it is true, and Alveric knew, that just as the glamour that brightens much of our lives, especially in early years, comes from rumours that reach us from Elfland by various messengers (on whom be blessings and peace), so there returns from our fields to Elfland again, to become a part of its mystery, all manner of little memories that we have lost and little devoted toys that were treasured once. And this is part of the law of ebb and flow that science may trace in all things; thus light grew the forest of coal, and the coal gives back light; thus rivers fill the sea, and the sea sends back to the rivers; thus all things give that receive; even Death.

Next Alveric saw lying there on the flat dry ground a toy that he yet remembered, which years and years ago (how could he say how many?) had been a childish joy to him, crudely carved out of wood; and one unlucky day it had been broken, and one unhappy day it had been thrown away. And now he saw it lying there not merely new and unbroken, but with a wonder about it, a splendour and a romance, the radiant transfigured thing that his young fancy had known. It lay there forsaken of Elfland as wonderful things of the sea lie sometimes desolate on wastes of sand, when the sea is a far blue bulk with a border of foam.

Dreary with lost romance was the plain from which Elfland had gone, though here and there Alveric saw again and again those little forsaken things that had been lost from his childhood, dropping through time to the ageless and hourless region of Elfland to be a part of its glory, and now left forlorn by this immense withdrawal. Old tunes, old songs, old voices, hummed there too, growing fainter and fainter, as though they could not live long in the fields we know.

And, when the sun set, a mauve-rose glow in the East, that Alveric fancied a little too gorgeous for Earth, led him onward still; for he deemed it to be the reflection cast on the sky by the glow of the splendour of Elfland. So he went on hoping to find it, horizon after horizon; and night came on with all Earth's comrade stars. And only then Alveric put aside at last that frantic restlessness that had driven him since the morning; and, wrapping himself in a loose cloak that he wore, ate such food as he had in a satchel, and slept a troubled sleep alone with other forsaken things.

At the earliest moment of dawn his impatience awoke him, although one of October's mists hid all glimpses of light. He ate the last of his food and then pushed on through the greyness.

No sound from the things of our fields came to him now; for men never went that way when Elfland was there, and none but Alveric went now to that desolate plain. He had travelled beyond the sound of cock-crow from the comfortable houses of men and was now marching through a curious silence, broken only now and then by the small dim cries of the lost songs that had been left by the ebb of Elfland and were fainter now than they had been the day before. And when dawn shone Alveric saw again so great a splendour in the sky, glowing all green low down in the south-east, that he thought once more he saw a reflection from Elfland, and pressed on hoping to find it over the next horizon. And he passed the next horizon; and still that shingly plain, and never a peak of the pale-blue Elfin Mountains.

Whether Elfland always lay over the next horizon, brightening the clouds with its glow, and moved away just as he came, or whether it had gone days or years before, he did not know but still kept on and on. And he came at last to a dry and grassless ridge on which his eyes and his hopes had been set for long, and from it he looked far over the desolate flatness that stretched to the rim of the sky, and saw never a sign of Elfland, never a slope of the mountains: even the little treasures of memory that had been left behind by the ebb were withering into things of our every day. Then Alveric drew his magical sword from its sheath. But though that sword had power against enchantment it had not been given the power to bring again an enchantment that was gone; and the desolate land remained the same, for all that he waved his sword, stony, deserted, unromantic and wide.

For a little while he went on; but in that flat land the horizon moved imperceptibly with him, and never a peak appeared of the Elfin Mountains; and on that dreary plain he soon discovered, as sooner or later many a man must, that he had lost Elfland.

Chapter XI

The Deep of the Woods

In those days Ziroonderel would amuse the boy by charms and by little wonders, and he was content for a while. And then he began to guess for himself, all in silence, where his mother was. He listened to all things said, and thought long about them. And days passed thus and he only knew she had gone, and still he said never a word of the thing with which his thoughts were busy. And then he came to know from things said or unsaid, or from looks or glances or wagging of heads, that there was a wonder about his mother's going. But what the wonder was he could not find, for all the marvels that crossed his mind when he guessed. And at last one day he asked Ziroonderel.

And stored though her old mind was with ages and ages of wisdom, and though she had feared this question, yet she did not know it had dwelt in his mind for days, and could find no better answer out of her wisdom than that his mother had gone to the woods. When the boy heard this he determined to go to the woods to find her.

Now in his walks abroad with Ziroonderel through the little hamlet of Erl, Orion would see the villagers walking by and the smith at his open forge, and folk in their doorways, and men that came in to the market from distant fields; and he knew them all. And most of all he knew Threl with his quiet feet, and Oth with his lithe limbs; for both of these would tell him tales when they met of the uplands, and the deep woods over the hill; and Orion on little journeys with his nurse loved to hear tales of far places.

There was an ancient myrtle tree by a well, where Ziroonderel would sit in the Summer evenings while Orion played on the grass; and Oth would cross the grass with his curious bow, going out in the evening, and sometimes Threl would come; and every time that one of them came Orion would stop him and ask for a tale of the woods. And if it were Oth he would bow to Ziroonderel with a look of awe as he bowed, and would tell some tale of what the deer did, and Orion would ask him why. Then a look would come over Oth's face as though he were carefully remembering things that had happened very long ago, and after some moments of silence he would give the ancient cause of whatever the deer did, which explained how they came by the custom.

If it were Threl that came across the grass he would appear not to see Ziroonderel and would tell his tale of the woods more hastily in a low voice and pass on, leaving the evening, as Orion felt, full of mystery behind him. He would tell tales of all manner of creatures; and the tales were so strange that he told them only to young Orion, because, as he explained, there were many folk that were unable to believe the truth, and he did not wish his tales to come to the ears of such. Once Orion had gone to his house, a dark hut full of skins: all kinds of skins hung on the wall, foxes, badgers, and martens; and there were smaller ones in heaps in the corners. To Orion Threl's dark hut was more full of wonder than any other house he had ever seen.

But now it was Autumn and the boy and his nurse saw Oth and Threl more seldom; for in the misty evenings with the threat of frost in the air they sat no longer by the myrtle tree. Yet Orion watched on their short walks; and one day he saw Threl going away from the village with his face to the uplands. And he called to Threl, and Threl stood still with a certain air of confusion, for he deemed himself of too little account to be clearly seen and noticed by the nurse at the castle, be she witch or woman. And Orion ran up to him and said "Show me the woods." And Ziroonderel perceived that the time had come when his thoughts were roaming beyond the lip of the valley, and knew that no spell of hers would hold him long from following after them. And Threl said, "No, my Master," and looked uneasily at Ziroonderel, who came after the boy and led him away from Threl. And Threl went on alone to his work in the deep of the woods.

And it was not otherwise than the witch had foreseen. For first Orion wept, and then he dreamed of the woods, and next day he slipped away alone to the house of Oth and asked him to take him with him when he went to hunt the deer. And Oth, standing on a wide deer-skin in front of blazing logs, spoke much of the woods, but did not take him then. Instead he brought Orion back to the Castle. And Ziroonderel regretted too late that she had idly said his mother was gone to the woods, for those words of hers had called up too soon that spirit of roving which was bound to come to him, and she saw that her spells could bring content no more. So in the end she let him go to the woods. But not until by lifting of wand and saying of incantation she had called the glamour of the woods down to the nursery hearth, and had made it haunt the shadows that went from the fire and creep with them all about the room, till the nursery was all as mysterious as the forest. When this spell would not soothe him and keep his longing at home she let him go to the woods.

He stole away once more to the house of Oth, over crisp grass one morning; and the old witch knew he had gone but did not call him back, for she had no spell to curb the love of roving in man, whether it came early or late. And she would not hold back his limbs when his heart was gone to the woods, for it is ever the way of witches with any two things to care for the more mysterious of the two. So the boy came alone to the house of Oth, through his garden where dead flowers hung on brown stalks, and the petals turned to slime if he fingered them, for November was come and the frosts were abroad all night. And this time Orion just met with a mood in Oth, which in less than an hour would have gone, that was favourable to the boy's longing. Oth was taking down his bow from the wall as Orion went in, and Oth's heart was gone to the woods; and when the boy came yearning to go to the woods too the hunter in that mood could not refuse him.

So Oth took Orion on his shoulder and went up out of the valley. Folk saw them go thus, Oth with his bow and his soft noiseless sandals, and his brown garments of leather, Orion on his shoulder, wrapped in the skin of a fawn which Oth had thrown round him. And as the village fell behind them Orion rejoiced to see the houses further and further away, for he had never been so far from them before. And when the uplands opened their distances to his eyes he felt that he was now upon no mere walk, but a journey. And then he saw the solemn gloom of the wintry woods far off, and that filled him at once with a delighted awe. To their darkness, their mystery and their shelter Oth brought him.

So softly Oth entered the wood that the blackbirds that guarded it, sitting watchful on branches, did not flee at his coming, but only uttered slowly their warning notes, and listened suspiciously till he passed, and were never sure if a man had broken the charm of the wood. Into that charm and the gloom and the deep silence Oth moved gravely; and a solemnness came on his face as he entered the wood; for to go on quiet feet through the wood was the work of his life, and he came to it as men come to their heart's desire. And soon he put the boy down on the brown bracken and went on for a while alone. Orion watched him go with his bow in his left hand, till he disappeared in the wood, like a shadow going to a gathering of shadows and merging amongst its fellows. And although Orion might not go with him now, he had great joy from this, for he knew by the way Oth went and the air he had that this was serious hunting and no mere amusement made to please a child; and it pleased him more than all the toys he had had. And quiet and lonely the great wood loomed round him while he waited for Oth to return.

And after a long while he heard a sound, all in the wonder of the wood, that was less loud than the sound that a blackbird made scattering dead leaves to find insects, and Oth had come back again.

He had not found a deer; and for a while he sat by Orion and shot arrows into a tree; but soon he gathered his arrows and took the boy on his shoulder again and turned homewards. And there were tears in Orion's eyes when they left the great wood; for he loved the mystery of the huge grey oaks, which we may pass by unnoticed or with but a momentary feeling of something forgotten, some message not quite given; but to him their spirits were playmates. So he came back to Erl as from new companions with his mind full of hints that he had from the wise old trunks, for to him each bole had a meaning. And Ziroonderel was waiting at the gateway when Oth brought Orion back; and she asked little of his time in the woods, and answered little when he told her of it, for she was jealous of them whose spell had lured him from hers. And all that night his dreams hunted deer in the deeps of the wood.

Next day he stole away again to the house of Oth. But Oth was away hunting, for he was in need of meat. So he went to the house of Threl. And there was Threl in his dark house amongst manifold skins. "Take me to the woods," said Orion. And Threl sat down in a wide wooden chair by his fire to think about it and to talk of the woods. He was not like Oth, speaking of a few simple things which he knew, of the deer, of the ways of the deer, and of the approach of the seasons; but he spoke of the things that he guessed in the deep of the wood and in the dark of time, the fables of men and of beasts; and especially he cared to tell the fables of the foxes and badgers, which he had come by from watching their ways at the falling of dusk. And as he sat there gazing into the fire, telling reminiscently of the ancient ways of the dwellers in bracken and bramble, Orion forgot his longing to go to the woods, and sat there on a small chair warm with skins, content. And to Threl he told what he had not said to Oth, how he thought that his mother might come one day round the trunk of one of the oak-trees, for she had gone for a while to the woods. And Threl thought that that might be; for there was nothing wonderful told of the woods that Threl thought unlikely.

And then Ziroonderel came for Orion and took him back to the Castle. And the next day she let him go to Oth again; and this time Oth took him once more to the wood. And a few days later he went again to Threl's dark house, in whose cobwebs and corners seemed to lurk the mystery of the forest, and heard Threl's curious tales.

And the branches of the forest grew black and still against the blaze of fierce sunsets, and Winter began to lay its spell on the uplands, and the wiser ones of the village prophesied snow. And one day Orion out in the woods with Oth saw the hunter shoot a stag. He watched him prepare it and skin it and cut it into two pieces and tie them up in the skin, with the head and horns hanging down. Then Oth fastened up the horns to the rest of the bundle and heaved it on to his shoulder, and with his great strength carried it home. And the boy rejoiced more than the hunter.

And that evening Orion went to tell the story to Threl, but Threl had more wonderful stories.

And so the days went by, while Orion drew from the forest and from the tales of Threl a love of all things that pertain to a hunter's calling, and a spirit grew in him that was well-matched with the name he bore; and nothing showed in him, yet, of the magical part of his lineage.

Chapter XII

The Unenchanted Plain

When Alveric understood that he had lost Elfland it was already evening and he had been gone two days and a night from Erl. For the second time he lay down for the night on that shingly plain whence Elfland had ebbed away: and at sunset the eastern horizon showed clear against turquoise sky, all black and jagged with rocks, without any sign of Elfland. And the twilight glimmered, but it was Earth's twilight, and not that dense barrier for which Alveric looked, which lies between Elfland and Earth. And the stars came out and were the stars we know, and Alveric slept below their familiar constellations.

He awoke in the birdless dawn very cold, hearing old voices crying faintly far off, as they slowly drifted away, like dreams going back to dreamland. He wondered if they would come to Elfland again, or if Elfland had ebbed too far. He searched all the horizon eastwards, and still saw nothing but the rocks of that desolate land. So he turned again toward the fields we know.

He walked back through the cold with all his impatience gone; and gradually some warmth came to him from walking, and later a little from the autumnal sun. He walked all day, and the sun was growing huge and red when he came again to the leather-worker's cottage. He asked for food, and the old man made him welcome: his pot was already simmering for his own evening meal: and it was not long before Alveric was sitting at the old table before a dish full of squirrels' legs, hedge-hogs and rabbit's meat. The old man would not eat till Alveric had eaten, but waited on him with such solicitude that Alveric felt that the moment of his opportunity was come, and turned to the old man as he offered him a piece of the back of a rabbit, and approached the subject of Elfland.

"The twilight is further away," said Alveric.

"Yes, yes," said the old man without any meaning in his voice, whatever he had in his mind.

"When did it go?" said Alveric.

"The twilight, master?" said his host.

"Yes," said Alveric.

"Ah, the twilight," the old man said.

"The barrier," said Alveric, and he lowered his voice, although he knew not why, "between here and Elfland."

At the word Elfland all comprehension faded out of the old man's eyes.

"Ah," he said.

"Old man," said Alveric, "you know where Elfland has gone."

"Gone?" said the old man.

That innocent surprise, thought Alveric, must be real; but at least he knew where it had been; it used to be only two fields away from his door.

"Elfland was in the next field once," said Alveric.

And the old man's eyes roved back into the past, and he gazed as it were on old days awhile, then he shook his head. And Alveric fixed him with his eye.

"You knew Elfland," he exclaimed.

Still the old man did not answer.

"You knew where the border was," said Alveric.

"I am old," said the leather-worker, "and I have no one to ask."

When he said that, Alveric knew that he was thinking of his old wife, and he knew too that had she been alive and standing there at that moment yet he would have had no news of Elfland: there seemed little more to say. But a certain petulance held him to the subject after he knew it to be hopeless.

"Who lives to the East of here?" he said.

"To the East?" the old man replied. "Master, are there not North and South and West that you needs must look to the East?"

There was a look of entreaty in his face but Alveric did not heed it. "Who lives to the East?" he said.

"Master, no one lives to the East," he answered. And that indeed was true.

"What used to be there?" said Alveric.

And the old man turned away to see to the stewing of his pot, and muttered as he turned, so that one hardly heard him.

"The past," he said.

No more would the old man say, nor explain what he had said. So Alveric asked him if he could have a bed for the night, and his host showed him the old bed he remembered across that vague number of years. And Alveric accepted the bed without more ado so as to let the old man go to his own supper. And very soon Alveric was deep asleep, warm and resting at last, while his host turned over slowly in his mind many things of which Alveric had supposed he knew nothing.

When the birds of our fields woke Alveric, singing late in the last of October, on a morning that reminded them of Spring, he rose and went out of doors, and went to the highest part of the little field that lay on the windowless side of the old man's house toward Elfland. There he looked eastward and saw all the way to the curved line of the sky the same barren, desolate, rocky plain that had been there yesterday and the day before. Then the leather-worker gave him breakfast, and afterwards he went out and looked again at the plain. And over his dinner, which his host timidly shared, Alveric neared once more the subject of Elfland. And something in the old man's sayings or silences made

Alveric hopeful that even yet he would have some news of the whereabouts of the pale-blue Elfin Mountains. So he brought the old man out and turned to the East, to which his companion looked with reluctant eyes; and pointing to one particular rock, the most noticeable and near, said, hoping for definite news of a definite thing, "How long has that rock been there?"

And the answer came to his hopes like hail to apple-blossom: "It is there and we must make the best of it."

The unexpectedness of the answer dazed Alveric; and when he saw that reasonable questions about definite things brought him no logical answer he despaired of getting practical information to guide his fantastic journey. So he walked on the eastward side of the cottage all the afternoon, watching the dreary plain, and it never changed or moved: no pale-blue mountains appeared, no Elfland came flooding back: and evening came and the rocks glowed dully with the low rays of the sun, and darkened when it set, changing with all Earth's changes, but with no enchantment of Elfland. Then Alveric decided on a great journey.

He returned to the cottage and told the leather-worker that he needed to buy much provisions, as much as he could carry. And over supper they planned what he should have. And the old man promised to go next day amongst the neighbours; telling of all the things he would get from each, and somewhat more if God should prosper his snaring. For Alveric had determined to travel eastward till he found the lost land.

And Alveric slept early, and slept long, till the last of his fatigue was gone which came from his pursuit of Elfland: the old man woke him as he came back from his snaring. And the creatures that he had snared the old man put in his pot and hung it over his fire, while Alveric ate his breakfast. And all the morning the leather-worker went from house to house amongst his neighbours, dwelling on little farms at the edge of the fields we know; and he got salted meats from some, bread from one, a cheese from another, and came back burdened to his house in time to prepare dinner.

And all the provender that burdened the old man Alveric shouldered in a sack, and some he put in his wallet; and he filled his water-bottle and two more besides that his host had made from large skins, for he had seen no streams at all in the desolate land; and thus equipped he walked some way from the cottage, and looked again at the land from which Elfland had ebbed. He came back satisfied that he could carry provisions for a fortnight.

And in the evening while the old man prepared pieces of squirrels' meat Alveric stood again on the windowless side of the cottage, gazing still across the lonely land, hoping always to see emerge from the clouds that were colouring at sunset, those serene pale-blue mountains;

and seeing never a peak. And the sun set, and that was the last of October.

Next morning Alveric made a good meal in the cottage; then took his heavy burden of provisions, and paid his host and started. The door of the cottage opened toward the West and the old man cordially saw him away from his door with godspeed and farewells, but he would not move round his house to watch him going eastward; nor would he speak of that journey: it was as though to him there were only three points of the compass.

The bright autumnal sun was not yet high when Alveric went from the fields we know to the land that Elfland had left and that nothing else went near, with his big sack over his shoulder and his sword at his side. The may trees of memory that he had seen were all withered now, and the old songs and voices that had haunted that land were all now faint as sighs; and there seemed to be fewer of them, as though some had already died or had struggled back to Elfland.

All that day Alveric travelled, with the vigour that waits at the beginning of journeys, which helped him on though he was burdened with so much provisions, and a big blanket that he wore like a heavy cloak round his shoulders; and he carried besides a bundle of firewood, and a stave in his right hand. He was an incongruous figure with his stave and his sack and his sword; but he followed one idea, one inspiration, one hope; and so shared something of the strangeness that all men have who do this.

Halting at noon to eat and rest he went slowly on again and walked till evening: even then he did not rest as he had intended, for when twilight fell and lay heavy along the eastern sky he continually rose from his resting and went a little further to see if it might not be that dense deep twilight that made the frontier of the fields we know, shutting them off from Elfland. But it was always earthly twilight, until the stars came out, and they were all the familiar stars that look on Earth. Then he lay down among those unrounded and mossless rocks, and ate bread and cheese and drank water; and as the cold of night began to come over the plain he lit a small fire with his scanty bundle of wood and lay close to it with his cloak and his blanket round him; and before the embers were black he was sound asleep.

Dawn came without sound of bird or whisper of leaves or grasses, dawn came in dead silence and cold; and nothing on all that plain gave a welcome back to the light.

If darkness had lain forever upon those angular rocks it were better, Alveric thought, as he saw their shapeless companies sullenly glowing; darkness were better now that Elfland was gone. And though the misery of that disenchanted place entered his spirit with the chill of the dawn, yet his fiery hope still shone, and gave him little time to eat by the cold black circle of his lonely fire before it hurried him onward easterly over the rocks. And all that morning he travelled on without the comradeship of a blade of grass. The golden birds that he had seen before had long since fled back to Elfland, and the birds of our fields and all living things we know shunned all that empty waste. Alveric travelled as much alone as a man who goes back in memory to revisit remembered scenes, and instead of remembered scenes he was in a place from which every glamour had gone. He travelled somewhat lighter than on the day before, but he went more wearily, for he felt more heavily now the fatigue of the previous day. He rested long at mid-day and then went on. The myriad rocks stretched on and slightly jagged the horizon, and all day there came no glimpse of the pale-blue mountains. That evening from his dwindling provision of wood Alveric made another fire; its little flame going up alone in that waste seemed somehow to reveal the monstrous loneliness. He sat by his fire and thought of Lirazel and would not give up hope, though a glance at those rocks might have warned him not to hope, for something in their chaotic look partook of the plain that bred them, and they hinted it to be infinite.

Chapter XIII

The Reticence of the Leather-Worker

It was many days before Alveric learned from the monotony of the rocks that one day's journey was the same as another, and that by no number of journeys would he bring any change to his rugged horizons, which were all drearily like the ones they replaced and never brought a view of the pale-blue mountains. He had gone, while his fortnight's provisions grew lighter and lighter, for ten days over the rocks: it was now evening and Alveric understood at last that if he travelled further and failed soon to see the peaks of the Elfin Mountains he would starve. So he ate his supper sparingly in the darkness, his bundle of firewood having long since been used, and abandoned the hope that had led him. And as soon as there was any light at all to show him where the East was he ate a little of what he had saved from his supper, and started his long tramp back to the fields of men, over rocks that seemed all the harsher because his back was to Elfland. All that day he ate and drank little, and by nightfall he still had left full provisions for four more days.

He had hoped to travel faster during these last days, if he should have to turn back, because he would travel lighter: he had given no thought to the power of those monotonous rocks to weary and to depress with their desolation when the hope that had somewhat illumined their grimness was gone: he had thought little of turning back at all, till the tenth evening came and no pale-blue mountains, and he

continue lasting for Elfland

suddenly looked at his provisions. And all the monotony of his homeward journey was broken only by occasional fears that he might not be able to come to the fields we know.

The myriad rocks lay larger and thicker than tombstones and not so carefully shaped, yet the waste had the look of a graveyard stretching over the world with unrecording stones above nameless heads. Chilled by the bitter nights, guided by blazing sunsets, he went on through the morning mists and the empty noons and weary birdless evenings. More than a week went by since he had turned, and the last of his water was gone, and still he saw no sign of the fields we know, or anything more familiar than rocks that he seemed to remember and which would have misled him northward, southward, or eastward, were it not for the red November sun that he followed and sometimes some friendly star. And then at last, just as the darkness fell blackening that rocky multitude, there showed westward over the rocks, pale at first against remnants of sunset, but growing more and more orange, a window under one of the gables of man. Alveric rose and walked towards it till the rocks in the darkness and weariness overcame him and he lay down and slept; and the little yellow window shone into his dreams and made forms of hope as fair as any that came from Elfland.

The house that he saw in the morning when he woke seemed impossible to be the one whose tiny light had held out hope and help to him in the loneliness; it seemed now too plain and common. He recognized it for a house not far from the one of the leather-worker. Soon he came to a pool and drank. He came to a garden in which a woman was working early, and she asked him whence he had come. "From the East," he said, and pointed, and she did not understand. And so he came again to the cottage from which he had started, to ask once more for hospitality from the old man who had housed him twice.

He was standing in his doorway as Alveric came, walking wearily, and again he made him welcome. He gave him milk and then food. And Alveric ate, and then rested all the day: it was not till evening he spoke. But when he had eaten and rested and he was at the table again, and supper was now before him and there was light and warmth, he felt all at once the need of human speech. And then he poured out the story of that great journey over the land where the things of man ceased, and where yet no birds or little beasts had come, or even flowers, a chronicle of desolation. And the old man listened to the vivid words and said nothing, making some comments of his own only when Alveric spoke of the fields we know. He heard with politeness but said never a word of the land from which Elfland had ebbed. It was indeed as though all the land to the East were delusion, and as though Alveric had been restored from it or had awoken from dream, and were now among reasonably daily things, and there was nothing to say of the things of dream. Certainly never a word would the old man say in recognition of Elfland, or of anything eighty yards East of his cottage door. Then Alveric went to his bed and the old man sat alone till his fire was low, thinking of what he had heard and shaking his head. And all the next day Alveric rested there or walked in the old man's autumn-smitten garden, and sometimes he tried again to speak with his host of his great journey in the desolate land, but got from him no admission that such lands were, checked always by his avoidance of the topic, as though to speak of these lands might bring them nearer.

And Alveric pondered on many reasons for this. Had the old man been to Elfland in his youth and seen something he greatly feared, perhaps barely escaping from death or an age-long love? Was Elfland a mystery too great to be troubled by human voices? Did these folk dwelling there at the edge of our world know well the unearthly beauty of all the glories of Elfland, and fear that even to speak of them might be a lure to draw them whither their resolution, barely perhaps, held them back? Or might a word said of the magical land bring it nearer, to make fantastic and elvish the fields we know? To all these ponderings of Alveric there was no answer.

And yet one more day Alveric rested, and after that he set out to return to Erl. He set out in the morning, and his host came with him out of his doorway, saying farewell and speaking of his journey home and of the affairs of Erl, which were food for gossip over many farmlands. And great was the contrast between the good man's approval that he showed thus for the fields we know, over which Alveric journeyed now, and his disapproval for those other lands whither Alveric's hopes still turned. And they parted, and the old man's farewells dwindled, and then he turned back into his house, rubbing his hands contentedly as he slowly went, for he was glad to see one who had looked toward the fantastic lands turn now to a journey across the fields we know.

In those fields the frost was master, and Alveric walked over the crisp grey grass and breathed the clear fresh air thinking little of his home or his son, but planning how even yet he might come to Elfland; for he thought that further North there might be a way, coming round perhaps behind the pale-blue mountains. That Elfland had ebbed too far for him to overtake it there he felt despairingly sure, but scarcely believed it had gone along the entire frontier of twilight, where Elfland touches Earth as far as poet has sung. Further North he might find the frontier, unmoved, lying sleepy with twilight, and come under the pale-blue mountains and see his wife again: full of these thoughts he went over the misty mellow fields.

And full of his dreams and plans about that phantasmal land he came in the afternoon to the woods that brood above Erl. He entered the wood, and deep though he was amongst thoughts that were far from there, he soon saw the smoke of a fire a little way off, rising grey among the dark oak-boles. He went towards it to see who was there,

and there were his son and Ziroonderel warming their hands at the fire.
"Where have you been?" called Orion as soon as he saw him.
"Upon a journey," said Alveric.
"Oth is hunting," Orion said, and he pointed in the direction
whence the wind was fanning the smoke. And Ziroonderel said
nothing, for she saw more in Alveric's eyes than any questions of hers
would have drawn from his tongue. Then Orion showed him a deer-
skin on which he was sitting. "Oth shot it," he said.

There seemed to be a magic all round that fire of big logs quietly
smouldering in the woods upon Autumn's discarded robe that lay
brilliant there; and it was not the magic of Elfland, nor had Ziroonderel
called it up with her wand: it was only a magic of the wood's very own.

And Alveric stood there for a while in silence, watching the boy
and the witch by their fire in the woods, and understanding that the
time was come when he must tell Orion things that were not clear to
himself and that were puzzling him even now. Yet he did not speak of
them then, but saying something of the affairs of Erl, turned and
walked on toward his castle, while Ziroonderel and the boy came back
later with Oth.

And Alveric commanded supper when he came to his gateway, and
ate it alone in the great hall that there was in the Castle of Erl, and all
the while he was pondering words to say. And then he went in the
evening up to the nursery and told the boy how his mother was gone for
a while to Elfland, to her father's palace (which may only be told of in
song). And, unheeding any words of Orion then, he held on with the
brief tale that he had come to tell, and told how Elfland was gone.

"But that cannot be," said Orion, "for I hear the horns of Elfland
every day."

"You can hear them?" Alveric said.

And the boy replied, "I hear them blowing at evening."

Chapter XIV

The Quest for the Elfin Mountains

Winter descended on Erl and gripped the forest, holding the small
twigs stiff and still: in the valley it silenced the stream; and in the fields
of the oxen the grass was brittle as earthenware, and the breath of the
beasts went up like the smoke of encampments. And Orion still went to
the woods whenever Oth would take him, and sometimes he went with
Threl. When he went with Oth the wood was full of the glamour of the
beasts that Oth hunted, and the splendour of the great stags seemed to
haunt the gloom of far hollows; but when he went with Threl a mystery
haunted the wood, so that one could not say what creature might not
appear, nor what haunted and hid by every enormous bole. What beasts

there were in the wood even Threl did not know: many kinds fell to his subtlety, but who knew if these were all?

And when the boy was late in the wood, on happy evenings, he would always hear as the sun went blazing down, rank on rank of the elfin horns blowing far away eastwards in the chill of the coming dusk, very far and faint, like reveillé heard in dreams. From beyond the woods they sounded, all those ringing horns, from beyond the downs, far over the furthest curve of them; and he knew them for the silver horns of Elfland. In all other ways he was human, and but for his power to hear those horns of Elfland, whose music rings but a yard beyond human hearing, and his knowledge of what they were; but for these two things he was as yet not more than a human child.

And how the horns of Elfland blew over the barrier of twilight, to be heard by any ear in the fields we know, I cannot understand; yet Tennyson speaks of them as heard "faintly blowing" even in these fields of ours, and I believe that by accepting all that the poets say while duly inspired our errors will be fewest. So, though Science may deny or confirm it, Tennyson's line shall guide me here.

Alveric in those days went through the village of Erl, with his thoughts far from there, moodily; and he stopped at many doors, and spoke and planned, with his eyes always fixed as it seemed on things no one else could see. He was brooding on far horizons, and the last, over which was Elfland. And from house to house he gathered a little band of men.

It was Alveric's dream to find the frontier further North, to travel on over the fields we know, always searching new horizons, till he came to some place from which Elfland had not ebbed; to this he determined to dedicate his days.

When Lirazel was with him amongst the fields we know, his thoughts had ever been to make her more earthly; but now that she was gone the thoughts of his own mind were becoming daily more elvish, and folk began to look sideways at his fantastic mien. Dreaming always of Elfland and of elvish things he gathered horses and provender and made for his little band so huge a store of provisions that those who saw it wondered. Many men he asked to be of that curious band, and few would go with him to haunt horizons, when they heard whither he went. And the first that he found to be of that band was a lad that was crossed in love; and then a young shepherd, well used to lonely spaces; then one that had heard a curious song that someone sang one evening: it had set his thoughts roving away to impossible lands, and so he was well content to follow his fancies. One huge full moon one summer had shone all a warm night long on a lad as he lay in the hay, and after that he had guessed or seen things that he said the moon showed him: whatever they were none else saw any such things in Erl: he also joined Alveric's band as soon as he asked him. It was many days before

Alveric found these four; and more he could not find but a lad that was
quite witless, and he took him to tend the horses, for he understood
horses well, and they understood him, though no human man or woman
could make him out at all, except his mother, who wept when Alveric
had his promise to go; for she said that he was the prop and support of
her age, and knew what storms would come and when the swallows
would fly, and what colours the flowers would come up from seeds she
sowed in her garden, and where the spiders would build their webs, and
the ancient fables of flies: she wept and said that there would be more
things lost by his going than ever folk guessed in Erl. But Alveric took
him away: many go thus.

And one morning six horses heaped and hung with provisions all
round their saddles waited at Alveric's gateway, with the five men that
were to roam with him as far as the world's edge. He had taken long
counsel with Ziroonderel, but she said that no magic of hers had power
to charm Elfland or to cross the dread will of its King; he therefore
commended Orion to her care, knowing well that though hers was but
simple or earthly magic, yet no magic likely to cross the fields we
know, nor curse nor rune directed against his boy, would be able to
thwart her spell; and for himself he trusted to the fortune that waits at
the end of long weary journeys. To Orion he spoke long, not knowing
how long that journey might be before he again found Elfland, nor how
easily he might return across the frontier of twilight. He asked the boy
what he desired of life.

"To be a hunter," said he.

"What will you hunt while I am over the hills?" said his father.

"Stags, like Oth," said Orion.

Alveric commended that sport, for he himself loved it.

"And some day I will go a long way over the hills and hunt
stranger things," said the boy.

"What kind of things," asked Alveric. But the boy did not know.

His father suggested different kinds of beasts.

"No, stranger than them," said Orion. "Stranger even than bears."

"But what will they be?" asked his father.

"Magic things," said the boy.

But the horses moved restlessly down below in the cold, so that
there was no time for more idle talk, and Alveric said farewell to the
witch and his son and strode away thinking little of the future, for all
was too vague for thought.

Alveric mounted his horse over the heaps of provisions, and all the
band of six men rode away. The villagers stood in the street to see them
go. All knew their curious quest; and when all had saluted Alveric and
all had called their farewells to the last of the riders, a hum of talk
arose. And in the talk was contempt of Alveric's quest, and pity, and
ridicule; and sometimes affection spoke and sometimes scorn; yet in

the hearts of all there was envy; for their reason mocked the lonely roving of that outlandish adventure, but their hearts would have gone.

And away rode Alveric out of the village of Erl with his company of adventurers behind him; a moonstruck man, a madman, a lovesick lad, a shepherd boy and a poet. And Alveric made Vand, the young shepherd, the master of his encampment, for he deemed him to be the sanest amongst his following; but there were disputes at once as they rode, before they came to make any encampment; and Alveric, hearing or feeling the discontent of his men, learned that on such a quest as his it was not the sanest but the maddest that should be given authority. So he named Niv, the witless lad, the master of his encampment; and Niv served him well till a day that was far thence, and the moonstruck man stood by Niv, and all were content to do the bidding of Niv, and all honoured Alveric's quest. And many men in numerous lands do saner things with less harmony.

They came to the uplands and rode over the fields, and rode till they came to the furthest hedges of men, and to the houses that they have built at the verge, beyond which even their thoughts refuse to fare. Through this line of houses at the edge of those fields, four or five in every mile, Alveric went with his queer company. The leather-worker's hut was far to the South. Now he turned northward to ride past the backs of the houses, over fields through which once the barrier of twilight had run, till he should find some place where Elfland might seem not to have ebbed so far. He explained this to his men, and the leading spirits, Niv, and Zend who was moonstruck, applauded at once; and Thyl, the young dreamer of songs, said the scheme was a wise one too; and Vand was carried away by the keen zeal of these three; and it was all one to Rannok the lover. And they had not gone far along the backs of the houses when the red sun touched the horizon, and they hastened to make an encampment by what remained of the light of that short winter's day. And Niv said they would build a palace like those of kings, and the idea fired Zend to work like three men, and Thyl helped eagerly; and they set up stakes and stretched blankets upon them and made a wall of brushwood, for they were but just outside the hedgerows, and Vand helped too with rough hurdles and Rannok toiled on wearily; and when all was finished Niv said that it was a palace. And Alveric went in and rested, while they lit a fire outside. And Vand cooked a meal for them all, which he did every day for himself upon lonely downs; and none could have cared for the horses better than Niv.

And as the gloaming faded away the cold of winter grew; and by the time that the first star shone there seemed nothing in all the night but bitter cold, yet Alveric's men lay down by their fire in their leathers and furs and slept, all but Rannok the lover.

To Alveric lying on furs in his shelter, watching red embers glowing beyond dark shapes of his men, the quest promised well: he

would go far North watching every horizon for any sign of Elfland: he
would go by the border of the fields we know, and always be near
provisions: and if he got no glimpse of the pale-blue mountains he
would go on till he found some field from which Elfland had not ebbed,
and so come round behind them. And Niv and Zend and Thyl had all
sworn to him that evening that before many days were gone they would
surely all find Elfland. Upon this thought he slept.

Chapter XV

The Retreat of the Elf King

When Lirazel blew away with the splendid leaves they dropped
one by one from their dance in the gleaming air, and ran on over fields
for a while, and then gathered by hedgerows and rested; but Earth that
pulls all things down had no hold on her, for the rune of the King of
Elfland had crossed its borders, calling her home. So she rode
carelessly the great north-west wind, looking down idly on the fields
we know, as she swept over them homewards. No grip had Earth on her
any longer at all; for with her weight (which is where Earth holds us)
were gone all her earthly cares. She saw without grief old fields
wherein she and Alveric walked once: they drifted by; she saw the
houses of men: these also passed; and deep and dense and heavy with
colour, she saw the border of Elfland.

A last cry Earth called to her with many voices, a child shouting,
rooks cawing, the dull lowing of cows, a slow cart heaving home; then
she was into the dense barrier of twilight, and all Earth's sounds
dimmed suddenly: she was through it and they ceased. Like a tired
horse falling dead our north-west wind dropped at the frontier; for no
winds blow in Elfland that roam over the fields we know. And Lirazel
slanted slowly onward and down, till her feet were back again on the
magical soil of her home. She saw full fair the peaks of the Elfin
Mountains, and dark underneath them the forest that guarded the Elf
King's throne. Above this forest were glimmering even now great
spires in the elfin morning, which glows with more sparkling splendour
than do our most dewy dawns, and never passes away.

Over the elfin land the elfin lady passed with her light feet,
touching the grasses as thistledown touches them when it comes down
to them and brushes their crests while a languid wind rolls it slowly
over the fields we know. And all the elvish and fantastic things, and the
curious aspect of the land, and the odd flowers and the haunted trees,
and the ominous boding of magic that hung in the air, were all so full of
memories of her home that she flung her arms about the first gnarled
gnome-like trunk and kissed its wrinkled bark.

And so she came to the enchanted wood; and the sinister pines that guarded it, with the watchful ivy leaning over their branches, bowed to Lirazel as she passed. Not a wonder in that wood, not a grim hint of magic, but brought back the past to her as though it had scarcely gone. It was, she felt, but yesterday morning that she had gone away; and it was yesterday morning still. As she passed through the wood the gashes of Alveric's sword were yet fresh and white on the trees.

And now a light began to glow through the wood, then flash upon flash of colours, and she knew they shone from the glory and splendour of flowers that girdled the lawns of her father. To these she came again; and her faint footprints that she had made as she left her father's palace, and wondered to see Alveric there, were not yet gone from the bended grass and the spiders' webs and the dew. There the great flowers glowed in the elfin light; while beyond them there twinkled and flashed, with the portal through which she had left it still open wide to the lawns, the palace that may not be told of but only in song. Thither Lirazel returned. And the Elf King, who heard by magic the tread of her soundless feet, was before his door to meet her.

His great beard almost hid her as they embraced: he had sorrowed for her long through that elfin morning. He had wondered, despite his wisdom; he had feared, for all his runes; he had yearned for her as human hearts may yearn, for all that he was of magic stock dwelling beyond our fields. And now she was home again and the elfin morning brightened over leagues of Elfland with the old Elf King's joy, and even a glow was seen upon slopes of the Elfin Mountains.

And through the flash and glimmer of the vast doorway they passed into the palace once more; the knight of the Elf King's guard saluted with his sword as they went, but dared not turn his head after Lirazel's beauty; they came again to the hall of the Elf King's throne, which is made of rainbows and ice; and the great King seated himself and took Lirazel on his knee; and a calm came down upon Elfland.

And for long through the endless elfin morning nothing troubled that calm; Lirazel rested after the cares of Earth, the Elf King sat there keeping the deep content in his heart, the knight of the guard remained at the salute, his sword's point downwards still, the palace glowed and shone: it was like a scene in some deep pool beyond the sound of a city, with green reeds and gleaming fishes and myriads of tiny shells all shining in the twilight on deep water, which nothing has disturbed through all the long summer's day. And thus they rested beyond the fret of time, and the hours rested around them, as the little leaping waves of a cataract rest when the ice calms the stream: the serene blue peaks of the Elfin Mountains above them stood like unchanging dreams.

Then like the noise of some city heard amongst birds in woods, like a sob heard amongst children that are all met to rejoice, like laughter amongst a company that weep, like a shrill wind in orchards amongst the early blossom, like a wolf coming over the downs where the sheep are asleep, there came a feeling into the Elf King's mood that one was coming towards them across the fields of Earth. It was Alveric with his sword of thunderbolt-iron, which somehow the old King sensed by its flavour of magic.

Then the Elf King rose, and put his left arm about his daughter, and raised his right to make a mighty enchantment, standing up before his shining throne which is the very centre of Elfland. And with clear resonance deep down in his throat he chaunted a rhythmic spell, all made of words that Lirazel never had heard before, some age-old incantation, calling Elfland away, drawing it further from Earth. And the marvellous flowers heard as their petals drank in the music, and the deep notes flooded the lawns; and all the palace thrilled, and quivered with brighter colours; and a charm went over the plain as far as the frontier of twilight, and a trembling went through the enchanted wood. Still the Elf King chaunted on. The ringing ominous notes came now to the Elfin Mountains, and all their line of peaks quivered as hills in haze, when the heat of summer beats up from the moors and visibly dances in air. All Elfland heard, all Elfland obeyed that spell. And now the King and his daughter drifted away, as the smoke of the nomads drifts over Sahara away from their camel's-hair tents, as dreams drift away at dawn, as clouds over the sunset; and like the wind with the smoke, night with the dreams, warmth with the sunset, all Elfland drifted with them. All Elfland drifted with them and left the desolate plain, the dreary deserted region, the unenchanted land. So swiftly that spell was uttered, so suddenly Elfland obeyed, that many a little song, old memory, garden or may tree of remembered years, was swept but a little way by the drift and heave of Elfland, swaying too slowly eastwards till the elfin lawns were gone, and the barrier of twilight heaved over them and left them among the rocks.

And whither Elfland went I cannot say, nor even whether it followed the curve of the Earth or drifted beyond our rocks out into twilight: there had been an enchantment near to our fields and now there was none: wherever it went it was far.

Then the Elf King ceased to chaunt and all was accomplished. As silently as, in a moment that none can determine, the long layers over the sunset turn from gold to pink, or from a glowing pink to a listless unlit colour, all Elfland left the edges of those fields by which its wonder had lurked for long ages of men, and was away now whither I know not. And the Elf King seated himself again on his throne of mist and ice, in which charmed rainbows were, and took Lirazel his daughter again on his knee, and the calm that his chaunting had broken came back heavy and deep over Elfland. Heavy and deep it fell on the lawns, heavy and deep on the flowers; each dazzling blade of grass was still in its little curve as though Nature in a moment of mourning said "Hush" at the sudden end of the world; and the flowers dreamed on in their beauty, immune from Autumn or wind. Far over the moors of the trolls slept the calm of the King of Elfland, where the smoke from their queer habitations hung stilled in the air; and in a forest wherein it quieted the trembling of myriads of petals on roses, it stilled the pools where the great lilies towered, till they and their reflections slept on in one gorgeous dream. And there below motionless fronds of dream-gripped trees, on the still water dreaming of the still air, where the huge lily-leaves floated green in the calm, was the troll Lurulu, sitting upon a leaf. For thus they named in Elfland the troll that had gone to Erl. He sat there gazing into the water at a certain impudent look that he had on. He gazed and gazed and gazed.

Nothing stirred, nothing changed. All things were still, reposing in the deep content of the King. The Knight of the Guard brought his sword back to the carry, and afterwards stood as still at his perpetual post as some suit of armour whose owner is centuries dead. And still the King sat silent with his daughter upon his knee, his blue eyes unmoving as the pale-blue peaks, which through wide windows shone from the Elfin Mountains.

And the Elf King stirred not, nor changed; but held to that moment in which he had found content; and laid its influence over all his dominions, for the good and welfare of Elfland; for he had what all our troubled world with all its changes seeks, and finds so rarely and must at once cast it away. He had found content and held it.

And in that calm that settled down upon Elfland there passed ten years over the fields we know.

Chapter XVI

Orion Hunts the Stag

There passed ten years over the fields we know; and Orion grew and learned the art of Oth, and had the cunning of Threl, and knew the woods and the slopes and vales of the downs, as many another boy knows how to multiply figures by other figures or to draw the thoughts from a language not his own and to set them down again in words of his own tongue. And little he knew of the things that ink may do, how it can mark a dead man's thought for the wonder of later years, and tell of happenings that are gone clean away, and be a voice for us out of the dark of time, and save many a fragile thing from the pounding of heavy ages; or carry to us, over the rolling centuries, even a song from lips long dead on forgotten hills. Little knew he of ink; but the touch of a roe deer's feet on dry ground, gone three hours, was a clear path to him, and nothing went through the woods but Orion read its story. And all the sounds of the wood were as full of clear meaning to him as are to the mathematician the signs and figures he makes when he divides his millions by tens and elevens and twelves. He knew by sun and moon and wind what birds would enter the wood, he knew of the coming seasons whether they would be mild or severe, only a little later than the beasts of the wood themselves, which have not human reason or soul and that know so much more than we.

And so he grew to know the very mood of the woods, and could enter their shadowy shelter like one of the woodland beasts. And this he could do when he was barely fourteen years; and many a man lives all his years and can never enter a wood without changing the whole mood of its shadowy ways. For men enter a wood perhaps with the wind behind them, they brush against branches, step on twigs; speak, smoke, or tread heavily; and jays cry out against them, pigeons leave the trees, rabbits pad off to safety, and far more beasts than they know slip on soft feet away from their coming. But Orion moved like Threl, in shoes of deer-skin with the tread of a hunter. And none of the beasts of the wood knew when he was come.

And he came to have a pile of skins like Oth, that he won with his bow in the wood; and he hung great horns of stags in the hall of the castle, high up among old horns where the spider had lived for ages. And this was one of the signs whereby the people of Erl came to know him now for their lord, for no news came of Alveric, and all the old lords of Erl had been hunters of deer. And another sign was the departing of the witch Ziroonderel when she went back to her hill; and Orion lived in the castle now by himself, and she dwelt in her cottage again where her cabbages grew on the high land near to the thunder.

And all that Winter Orion hunted the stags in the wood, but when Spring came he put his bow away. Yet all through the season of song and flowers his thoughts were still with the chase; and he went from house to house wherever a man had one of the long thin dogs that hunt. And sometimes he bought the dog, and sometimes the man would promise to lend it on days of hunting. Thus Orion formed a pack of brown long-haired hounds and yearned for the Spring and Summer to go by. And one Spring evening when Orion was tending his hounds, when villagers were mostly at their doors to notice the length of the evening, there came a man up the street whom nobody knew. He came from the uplands, wrapped in the most aged of clothes, which clung to him as though they had clung forever, and were somehow a part of him and yet part of the Earth, for they were mellowed by the clay of the high fields to its own deep brown. And folk noticed the easy stride of a mighty walker, and a weariness in his eyes: and none knew who he was.

And then a woman said "It is Vand that was only a lad." And they all crowded about him then, for it was indeed Vand who had left the sheep more than ten years ago to ride with Alveric no one in Erl knew whither. "How fares our master?" they said. And a look of weariness came in the eyes of Vand.

"He follows the quest," he said.

"Whither?" they asked.

"To the North," he said. "He seeks for Elfland still."

"Why have you left him?" they asked.

"I lost the hope," he said.

They questioned him no more then, for all men knew that to seek for Elfland one needed a strong hope, and without it one saw no gleam of the Elfin Mountains, serene with unchanging blue. And then the mother of Niv came running up. "Is it indeed Vand?" she said. And they all said "Yes, it is Vand."

And while they murmured together about Vand, and of how years and wandering had changed him, she said to him, "Tell me of my son." And Vand replied "He leads the quest. There is none whom my master trusts more." And they all wondered, and yet they had no cause for wonder, for it was a mad quest.

But Niv's mother alone did not wonder. "I knew he would," she said. "I knew he would." And she was filled with a great content.

There are events and seasons to suit the mood of every man, though few indeed could have suited the crazed mood of Niv, yet there came Alveric's quest of Elfland, and so Niv found his work.

And talking in the late evening with Vand the folk of Erl heard tales of many camps, many marches, a tale of profitless wandering where Alveric haunted horizons year after year like a ghost. And sometimes out of Vand's sadness that had come from those profitless years a smile would shine as he told of some foolish happening that had taken place in the camp. But all was told by one that had lost hope in the quest. This was not the way to tell of it, not with doubts, not with smiles. For such a quest may only be told of by those who are fired by its glory: from the mad brain of Niv or the moonstruck wits of Zend we might have news of that quest which could light our minds with some gleam of its meaning; but never from the story, be it made out of facts or scoffs, told by one whom the quest itself was able to lure no longer. The stars stole out and still Vand was telling his stories, and one by one the people went back to their houses, caring to hear no more of the hopeless quest. Had the tale been told by one who clung yet to the faith that still was leading Alveric's wanderers on, the stars would have weakened before those folk left the teller, the sky would have brightened so widely before they left him that one would have said at last "Why! It is morning." Not till then would they have gone.

And the next day Vand went back to the downs and the sheep and troubled himself with romantic quests no more.

And during that Spring men spoke of Alveric again, wondering awhile at his quest, speaking awhile of Lirazel, and guessing where she had gone, and guessing why; and where they could not guess telling some tale to explain all, which went from mouth to mouth till they came to believe it. And Spring went by and they forgot Alveric and obeyed the will of Orion.

And then one day as Orion was waiting for the Summer to go by, with his heart on frosty days and his dreams with his hounds on the uplands, Rannok the lover came over the downs by the path by which Vand had come, and walked down into Erl. Rannok with his heart free at last, with all his melancholy gone, Rannok without woe, careless, care-free, content, looking only for rest after his long wandering, sighing no more. And nothing but this would have made Vyria care to have him, the girl he had sought once. So the end of this was that she married him, and he too went roaming no more on fantastic quests.

And though some looked to the uplands through many an evening, till the long days wore away and a strange wind touched the leaves, and some peered over the further curves of the downs, yet they saw none more of the followers of Alveric's quest coming back by the path that Vand and Rannok had trod. And by the time that the leaves were a wonder of scarlet and gold men spoke no more of Alveric but obeyed Orion his son.

And in this season Orion arose one day before dawn and took his horn and his bow and went to his hounds, who wondered to hear his step before light was come: they heard it all in their sleep and awoke and clamoured to him. And he loosed them and calmed them and led them away to the downs. And to the lonely magnificence of the downs they came when the stags are feeding on dewy grasses, before men are awake. All in the wild wet morning they ran over the gleaming slopes, Orion and his hounds, all rejoicing together. And the scent of the thyme came heavy with the air that Orion breathed, as he trod its wide patches blooming late in the year. To the hounds there came all the wandering scents of the morning. And what wild creatures had met on the hill in the dark and what had crossed it going upon their journeys, and whither all had gone when the day grew bright, bringing the threat of man, Orion guessed and wondered; but to the hounds all was clear. And some of the scents they noted with careful noses, and some they scorned, and for one they sought in vain, for the great red deer were not on the downs that morning.

And Orion led them far from the Vale of Erl but saw no stag that day, and never a wind brought the scent that the anxious hounds were seeking, nor could they find it hidden in any grass or leaves. And evening came on him bringing his hounds home, calling on stragglers with his horn, while the sun turned huge and scarlet; and fainter than echoes of his horn, and far beyond downs and mist, but clear each silver note, he heard the elfin horns that called to him always at evening.

With the great comradeship of a common weariness he and his

hounds came home dark in the starlight. The windows of Erl at last flashed to them the glow of their welcome. Hounds came to their kennels and ate, and lay down to contented sleep: Orion went to his castle. He too ate, and afterwards sat thinking of the downs and his hounds and the day, his mind lulled by fatigue to that point at which it rests beyond care.

And many a day passed thus. And then one dewy morning, coming over a ridge of the downs, they saw a stag below them feeding late when all the rest were gone. The hounds all broke into one joyous cry, the heavy stag moved nimbly over the grass, Orion shot an arrow and missed; all these things happened in a moment. And then the hounds streamed away, and the wind went over the backs of them with a ripple, and the stag went away as though every one of his feet were on little dancing springs. And at first the hounds were swifter than Orion, but he was as tireless as they, and by taking sometimes shorter ways than theirs he stayed near them till they came to a stream and faltered and began to need the help of human reason. And such help as human reason can give in such a matter Orion gave them, and soon they were on again. And the morning passed as they went from hill to hill, and they had not seen the stag a second time; and the afternoon wore away, and still the hounds followed every step of the stag with a skill as strange as magic. And towards evening Orion saw him, going slowly, along the slope of a hill, over coarse grass that was shining in the rays of the low sun. He cheered on his hounds and they ran him over three more small valleys, but down at the bottom of the third he turned round amongst the pebbles of a stream and waited there for the hounds. And they came baying round him, watching his brow antlers. And there they tore him down and killed him at sunset. And Orion wound his horn with a great joy in his heart: he wanted no more than this. And with a note like that of joy, as though they also rejoiced, or mocked his rejoicing, over hills that he knew not, perhaps from the far side of the sunset, the horns of Elfland answered.

Chapter XVII

The Unicorn Comes in the Starlight

And winter came, and whitened the roofs of Erl, and all the forest and uplands. And when Orion took his hounds afield in the morning the world lay like a book that was newly written by Life; for all the story of the night before lay in long lines in the snow. Here the fox had gone and there the badger, and here the red deer had gone out of the wood; the tracks led over the downs and disappeared from sight, as the deeds of statesmen, soldiers, courtiers and politicians appear and disappear on the pages of history. Even the birds had their record on those white downs, where the eye could follow each step of their treble claws, till suddenly on each side of the track would appear three little scars where the tips of their longest feathers had flicked the snow, and there the track faded utterly. They were like some popular cry, some vehement fancy, that comes down on a page of history for a day, and passes, leaving no other record at all except those lines on one page.

And amongst all these records left of the story of night Orion would choose the track of some great stag not too long gone, and would follow it with his hounds away over the downs until even the sound of his horn could be heard no longer in Erl. And over a ridge with his hounds, he and they all black against red remnants of sunset, the folk of Erl would see him coming home; and often it was not until all the stars were glowing through the frost. Often the skin of a red deer hung over his shoulders and the huge horns bobbed and nodded above his head.

And at this time there met one day in the forge of Narl, all unknown to Orion, the men of the parliament of Erl. They met after sunset when all were home from their work. And gravely Narl handed to each the mead that was brewed from the clover honey; and when all were come they sat silent. And then Narl broke the silence, saying that Alveric ruled over Erl no more and his son was Lord of Erl, and telling again how once they had hoped for a magic lord to rule over the valley and to make it famous, and saying that this should be he. "And where now," he said, "is the magic for which we hoped? For he hunts the deer as all his forefathers hunted, and nothing of magic has touched him from over there; and there is no new thing."

And Oth stood up to defend him. "He is as fleet as his hounds," he said, "and hunts from dawn to sunset, and crosses the furthest downs and comes home untired."

"It is but youth," said Guhic. And so said all but Threl.

And Threl stood up and said: "He has a knowledge of the ways of the woods, and the lore of the beasts, beyond the learning of man."

"You taught him," said Guhic. "There is no magic here."

"Nothing of this," said Narl, "is from over there."

Thus they argued awhile lamenting the loss of the magic for which they had hoped: for never a valley but history touches it once, never a village but once its name is awhile on the lips of men; only the village of Erl was utterly unrecorded; never a century knew it beyond the round of its downs. And now all their plans seemed lost which they made so long ago, and they saw no hope except in the mead that was brewed from the clover honey. To this they turned in silence. Now it was a goodly brew.

And in a while new plans flashed clear in their minds, new schemes, new devices; and debates in the parliament of Erl flowed proudly on. And they would have made a plan and a policy; but Oth arose from his seat. There was in a flint-built house in the village of Erl an ancient Chronicle, a volume bound in leather, and in it at certain seasons folk wrote all manner of things, the wisdom of farmers concerning the time to sow, the wisdom of hunters concerning the tracking of stags, and the wisdom of prophets that told of the way of Earth. From this Oth quoted now, two lines that he remembered on one of the aged pages; and all the rest of that page told of hoeing; these lines he said to the parliament of Erl as they sat with the mead before them at their table:

"Hooded, and veiled with their night-like tresses,
    The Fates shall bring what no prophet guesses."

And then they planned no more, for either their minds were calmed by a certain awe that they seemed to find in the lines, or it may be the mead was stronger than anything written in books. However it be they sat silent over their mead. And in early starlight while the West still glowed they passed away from Narl's house back to their own homes grumbling as they went that they had no magic lord to rule over Erl, and yearning for magic, to save from oblivion the village and valley they loved. They parted one by one as they came to their houses. And three or four that dwelt near the end of the village on the side that was under the downs were not yet come to their doors, when, white and clear in the starlight and what remained of the gloaming, they saw hard-pressed and wearied a hunted unicorn coming across the downs. They stopped and gazed and shaded their eyes and stroked their beards and wondered. And still it was a white unicorn galloping wearily. And then they heard drawing nearer the cry of Orion's hounds.

Chapter XVIII

The Grey Tent in the Evening

On the day that the hunted unicorn crossed the valley of Erl Alveric had wandered for over eleven years. For more than ten years, a company of six, they went by the backs of the houses by the edge of the fields we know, and camped at evenings with their queer material hung greyly on poles. And whether or not the strange romance of their quest mirrored itself in all the things about them, those camps of theirs seemed always the strangest thing in the landscape; and as evening grew greyer around them their romance and mystery grew.

And for all the vehemence of Alveric's ambition they travelled leisurely and lazily: sometimes in a pleasant camp they stayed for three days; then they went strolling on. Nine or ten miles they would march and then they would camp again. Someday, Alveric felt sure in his heart, they would see that border of twilight, someday they would enter

Elfland. And in Elfland he knew that time was not as here: he would meet Lirazel unaged in Elfland, with never one smile lost to the raging years, never a furrow worn by the ruin of time. This was his hope; and it led his queer company on from camp to camp, and cheered them round the fire in the lonely evenings, and brought them far to the North, travelling all along the edge of the fields we know, where all men's faces turned the other way, and the six wanderers went unseen and unheeded. Only the mind of Vand hung back from their hope, and more and more every year his reason denied the lure that was leading the rest. And then one day he lost his faith in Elfland. After that he only followed until a day when the wind was full of rain, and all were cold and wet and the horses weary; he left them then.

And Rannok followed because he had no hope in his heart and wished to wander from sorrow; until one day when all the blackbirds were singing in trees of the fields we know, and his hopelessness left him in the glittering sunshine, and he thought of the cosy homes and the haunts of men. And soon he too passed out of the camp one evening and set off for the pleasant lands.

And now the four that were left were all of one mind, and under the wet coarse cloth that they hung on poles there was deep content in the evenings. For Alveric clung to his hope with all the strength of his race, that had once won Erl in old battles and held it for centuries long, and in the vacant minds of Niv and Zend this idea grew strong and big, like some rare flower that a gardener may plant by chance in a wild untended place. And Thyl sung of the hope; and all his wild fancies that roamed after song decked Alveric's quest with more and more of glamour. So all were of one mind. And greater quests whether mad or sane have prospered when this was so, and greater quests have failed when it was otherwise.

They had gone northwards for years along the backs of those houses; and then one day they would turn eastwards, wherever a certain look in the sky or a touch of weirdness at evening, or a mere prophecy of Niv's, seemed to suggest a proximity of Elfland. Upon such occasions they would travel over the rocks, that for all those years lay bordering the fields we know, until Alveric saw that provisions for men and horses would barely bring them back to the houses of men. Then he would turn again, but Niv would have led them still onward over the rocks, for his enthusiasm grew as they went; and Thyl sang to them prophesying success; and Zend would say that he saw the peaks and the spires of Elfland; only Alveric was wise. And so they would come to the houses of men again, and buy more provisions. And Niv and Zend and Thyl would babble of the quest, pouring out the enthusiasm that burned in their hearts; but Alveric did not speak of it, for he had learned that men in those fields neither speak of nor look towards Elfland, although he had not learned why.

Soon they were on again, and the folk that had sold them the produce of fields we know gazed curiously after them as they went, as though they thought that from madness alone or from dreams inspired by the moon came all the talk they had heard from Niv and Zend and Thyl.

Thus they always travelled on, always seeking new points from which to discover Elfland; and on the left of them blew scents from the fields we know, the scent of lilac from cottage gardens in May, and then the scent of the white-thorn and then of roses, till all the air was heavy with new-mown hay. They heard the low of cattle away on their left, heard human voices, heard partridges calling; heard all the sounds that go up from happy farms; and on their right was always the desolate land, always the rocks and never grass nor a flower. They had the companionship of men no more, and yet they could not find Elfland. In such a case they needed the songs of Thyl and the sure hope of Niv.

And the talk of Alveric's quest spread through the land and overtook his wanderings, till all men that he passed by knew his story; and from some he had the contempt that some men give to those who dedicate all their days to a quest, and from others he had honour; but all he asked for was provender, and this he bought when they brought it. So they went on. Like legendary things they passed along the backs of the houses, putting up their grey shapeless tent in the grey evenings. They came as quietly as rain, and went away like mists drifting. There were jests about them and songs. And the songs outlasted the jests. At last they became a legend, which haunted those farms for ever: they were spoken of when men told of hopeless quests, and held up to laughter or glory, whichever men had to give.

And all the while the King of Elfland watched; for he knew by magic when Alveric's sword drew near: it had troubled his kingdom once, and the King of Elfland knew well the flavour of thunderbolt iron when he felt it loom on the air. From this he had withdrawn his frontiers far, leaving all that ragged land deserted of Elfland; and though he knew not the length of human journeys, he had left a space that to cross would weary the comet, and rightly deemed himself safe.

But when Alveric with his sword was far to the North the Elf King loosened the grip with which he had withdrawn Elfland, as the Moon that withdraws the tide lets it flow back again, and Elfland came racing back as the tide over flat sands. With a long ribbon of twilight at its edge it floated back over the waste of rocks; with old songs it came, with old dreams, and with old voices. And in a while the frontier of twilight lay flashing and glimmering near the fields we know, like an endless Summer evening that lingered on out of the golden age. But bleak and far to the North where Alveric wandered the limitless rocks still heaped the desolate land; only to fields from which he and his sword and his adventurous band were remotely gone that mighty inlet of Elfland came lapping back. So that close again to the leather-worker's cottage and to the farms of his neighbours, a bare three fields away, lay the land that was heaped and piled with all the wonder for which poets seek so hard, the very treasury of all romantic things; and the Elfin Mountains gazed over the border serenely, as though their pale-blue peaks had never moved. And here the unicorns fed along the border as it was their custom to do, feeding sometimes in Elfland, which is the home of all fabulous things, cropping lilies below the slopes of the Elfin Mountains, and sometimes slipping through the border of twilight at evening when all our fields are still, to feed upon earthly grass. It is because of this craving for earthly grass that comes on them now and then, as the red deer in Highland mountains crave once a year for the sea, that, fabulous though they are on account of their birth in Elfland, their existence is nevertheless known among men. The fox, which is born in our fields, also crosses the frontier, going into the border of twilight at certain seasons; it is thence that he gets the romance with which he comes back to our fields. He also is fabulous, but only in Elfland, as the unicorns are fabulous here.

And seldom the folk on those farms saw the unicorns, even dim in the gloaming, for their faces were turned forever away from Elfland. The wonder, the beauty, the glamour, the story of Elfland were for minds that had leisure to care for such things as these; but the crops needed these men, and the beasts that were not fabulous, and the thatch, and the hedges and a thousand things: barely at the end of each year they won their fight against Winter: they knew well that if they let a thought of theirs turn but for a moment towards Elfland, its glory would grip them soon and take all their leisure away, and there would be no time left to mend thatch or hedge or to plough the fields we know. But Orion lured by the sound of the horns that blew from Elfland at evening, and that some elvish attuning of his ears to magical things caused him alone in all those fields to hear, came with his hounds to a field across which ran the frontier of twilight, and found the unicorns there late on an evening. And, slipping along a hedge of the little field with his hounds padding behind him, he came between a unicorn and the frontier and cut it off from Elfland. This was the unicorn that with flashing neck, covered with flecks of foam that shone silvery in the starlight, panting, harried and weary, came across the valley of Erl, like an inspiration, like a new dynasty to a custom-weary land, like news of a happier continent found far-off by suddenly returned sea-faring men.

Chapter XIX

Twelve Old Men Without Magic

Now few things pass by a village and leave no talk behind them. Nor did this unicorn. For the three that saw it going by in the starlight immediately told their families, and many of these ran from their houses to tell the good news to others, for all strange news was accounted good in Erl, because of the talk that it made; and talk was held to be needful when work was over to pass the evenings away. So they talked long of the unicorn.

And, after a day or two, in the forge of Narl the parliament of Erl was met again, seated by mugs of mead, discussing the unicorn. And some rejoiced and said that Orion was magic, because unicorns were of magic stock and came from beyond our fields.

"Therefore," said one, "he has been to lands of which it does not become us to speak, and is magic, as all things are which dwell over there."

And some agreed and held that their plans had come to fruition.

But others said that the beast went by in the starlight, if beast it were, and who could say it was a unicorn? And one said that in the starlight it was hard to see it at all, and another said unicorns were hard to recognize. And then they began to discuss the size and shape of these beasts, and all the known legends that told of them, and came no nearer to agreeing together whether or not their lord had hunted a unicorn. Till at last Narl seeing that they would not thus come by the truth, and deeming it necessary that the fact should be established one way or the other forever, rose up and told them that the time had come for the vote. So by a method they had of casting shells of various colours into a horn that was passed from man to man, they voted about the unicorn as Narl had commanded. And a hush fell, and Narl counted. And it was seen to have been established by vote that there had been no unicorn.

Sorrowfully then that parliament of Erl saw that their plans to have a magic lord had failed; they were all old men, and the hope that they had had for so long being gone they turned less easily to newer plans than they had to the plan that they made so long ago. What should they do now, they said? How come by magic? What could they do that the world should remember Erl? Twelve old men without magic. They sat there over their mead, and it could not lighten their sadness.

But Orion was away with his hounds near that great inlet of Elfland where it lay as it were at high tide, touching the very grass of the fields we know. He went there at evening when the horns blew clear to guide him, and waited there all quiet at the edge of those fields for the unicorns to steal across the border. For he hunted stags no more.

And as he went over those fields in the late afternoon folk working on the farms would greet him cheerily; but when still he went eastwards they spoke to him less and less, till at last when he neared the border and still kept on they looked his way no more, but left him and his hounds to their own devices.

And by the time the sun set he would be standing quiet by a hedge that ran right down into the frontier of twilight, with his hounds all gathered close in under the hedge, with his eye on them all lest one of them dared to move. And the pigeons would come home to trees of the fields we know, and twittering starlings; and the elfin horns would blow, clear silver magical music thrilling the chilled air, and all the colours of clouds would go suddenly changing; it was then in the failing light, in the darkening of colours, that Orion would watch for a dim white shape stepping out of the border of twilight. And this evening just as he hushed a hound with his hand, just as all our fields went dim, there slipped a great white unicorn out of the border, still munching lilies such as never grew in any fields of ours. He came, a whiteness on perfectly silent feet, four or five yards into the fields we know, and stood there still as moonlight, and listened and listened and listened. Orion never moved, and he kept his hounds silent by some power he had or by some wisdom of theirs. And in five minutes the unicorn made a step or two forward, and began to crop the long sweet earthly grasses. And as soon as he moved there came others through the deep blue border of twilight, and all at once there were five of them feeding there. And still Orion stood with his hounds and waited.

Little by little the unicorns moved further away from the border, lured further and further into the fields we know by the deep rich earthly grasses, on which all five of them browsed in the silent evening. If a dog barked, even if a late cock crew, up went all their ears at once and they stood watchful, not trusting anything in the fields of men, or venturing into them far.

But at last the one that had come first through the twilight got so far from his magical home that Orion was able to run between him and the frontier, and his hounds came behind him. And then had Orion been toying with the chase, then had he hunted but for an idle whim, and not for that deep love of the huntsman's craft that only huntsmen know, then had he lost everything: for his hounds would have chased the nearest unicorns, and they would have been in a moment across the frontier and lost, and if the hounds had followed they would have been lost too, and all that day's work would have gone for nothing. But Orion led his hounds to chase the furthest, watching all the while to see if any hound would try to pursue the others; and only one began to, but Orion's whip was ready. And so he cut his quarry off from its home, and his hounds for the second time were in full cry after a unicorn.

As soon as the unicorn heard the feet of the hounds, and saw with one flash of his eye that he could not get to his enchanted home, he shot forward with a sudden spring of his limbs and went like an arrow over the fields we know. When he came to hedges he did not seem to gather his limbs to leap but seemed to glide over them with motionless muscles, galloping again when he touched the grass once more.

In that first rush the hounds drew far ahead of Orion, and this enabled him to head the unicorn off whenever it tried to turn to the magical land; and at such turnings he came near his hounds again. And the third time that Orion turned the unicorn it galloped straight away, and so continued over the fields of men. The cry of the hounds went through the calm of the evening like a long ripple across a sleeping lake following the unseen way of some strange diver. In that straight gallop the unicorn gained so much on the hounds that soon Orion only saw him far off, a white spot moving along a slope in the gloaming. Then it reached the top of a valley and passed from view. But that strong queer scent that led the hounds like a song remained clear on the grass, and they never checked or faltered except for a moment at streams. Even there their ranging noses picked up the magical scent before Orion came up to give them his aid.

And as the hunt went on the daylight faded away, till the sky was all prepared for the coming of stars. And one or two stars appeared, and a mist came up from streams and spread all white over fields, till they could not have seen the unicorn if he had been close before them. The very trees seemed sleeping. They passed by little houses, lonely, sheltered by elms; shut off by high hedges of yew from those that roamed the fields; houses that Orion had never seen or known till the chance course of this unicorn brought him suddenly past their doors. Dogs barked as they passed, and continued barking long, for that magical scent on the air and the rush and the voice of the pack told them something strange was afoot; and at first they barked because they would have shared in what was afoot, and afterwards to warn their masters about the strangeness. They barked long through the evening.

And once, as they passed a little house in a cluster of old thorns, a door suddenly opened, and a woman stood gazing to see them go by: she could have seen no more than grey shapes, but Orion in the moment as he passed saw all the glow of the house, and the yellow light streaming out into the cold. The merry warmth cheered him, and he would have rested awhile in that little oasis of man in the lonely fields, but the hounds went on and he followed; and those in the houses heard their cry go past like the sound of a trumpet whose echoes go fading away amongst the furthest hills.

A fox heard them coming, and stood quite still and listened: at first he was puzzled. Then he caught the scent of the unicorn, and all was clear to him, for he knew by the magic flavour that it was something coming from Elfland.

But when sheep caught the scent they were terrified, and ran all huddled together until they could run no more.

Cattle leaped up from their sleep, gazed dreamily, and wondered; but the unicorn went through them and away, as some rose-scented breeze that has strayed from valley gardens into the streets of a city slips through the noisy traffic and is gone.

Soon all the stars were looking on those quiet fields through which the hunt went with its exultation, a line of vehement life cleaving through sleep and silence. And now the unicorn, far out of sight though he was, no longer gained a little at every hedge. For at first he lost no more pace at any hedge than a bird loses passing clear of a cloud, while the great hounds struggled through what gaps they could find, or lay on their sides and wriggled between the stems of the bushes. But now he gathered his strength with more effort at every hedge, and sometimes hit the top of the hedge and stumbled. He was galloping slower too; for this was a journey such as no unicorn made through the deep calm of Elfland. And something told the tired hounds they were drawing nearer. And a new joy entered their voices.

They crossed a few more black hedges, and then there loomed before them the dark of a wood. When the unicorn entered the wood the voices of the hounds were clear in his ears. A pair of foxes saw him going slowly, and they ran along beside him to see what would befall the magic creature coming weary to them from Elfland. One on each side they ran, keeping his slow pace and watching him, and they had no fear of the hounds though they heard their cry, for they knew that nothing that followed that magical scent would turn aside after any earthly thing. So he went labouring through the wood, and the foxes watched him curiously all the way.

The hounds entered the wood and the great oaks rang with the sound of them, and Orion followed with an enduring speed that he may have got from our fields or that may have come to him over the border from Elfland. The dark of the wood was intense but he followed his hounds' cry, and they did not need to see with that wonderful scent to guide them. They never wavered as they followed that scent, but went on through gloaming and starlight. It was not like any hunt of fox or stag; for another fox will cross the line of a fox, or a stag may pass through a herd of stags and hinds; even a flock of sheep will bewilder hounds by crossing the line they follow; but this unicorn was the only magical thing in all our fields that night, and his scent lay unmistakable over the earthly grass, a burning pungent flavour of enchantment among the things of every day. They hunted him clear through the wood and down to a valley, the two foxes keeping with him and watching still: he picked his feet carefully as he went down the hill, as though his weight hurt them while he descended the slope, yet his pace was as fast as that of the hounds going down: then he went a little way along the trough of the valley, turning to his left as soon as he came down the hill, but the hounds gained on him then and he turned for the opposite slope. And then his weariness could be concealed no longer, the thing that all wild creatures conceal to the last; he toiled over every step as though his legs dragged his body heavily. Orion saw him from the opposite slope.

And when the unicorn got to the top the hounds were close behind him, so that he suddenly whipped round his great single horn and stood before them threatening. Then the hounds bayed about him, but the horn waved and bowed with such swift grace that no hound got a grip; they knew death when they saw it, and eager though they were to fasten upon him they leaped back from that flashing horn. Then Orion came up with his bow, but he would not shoot, perhaps because it was hard to put an arrow safely past his pack of hounds, perhaps because of a feeling such as we have to-day, and which is no new thing among us, that it was unfair to the unicorn. Instead he drew an old sword that he was wearing, and advanced through his hounds and engaged that deadly horn. And the unicorn arched his neck, and the horn flashed at Orion; and, weary though the unicorn was, yet a mighty force remained in that muscular neck to drive the blow that he aimed, and Orion barely parried. He thrust at the unicorn's throat, but the great horn tossed the sword aside from its aim and again lunged at Orion. Again he parried with the whole weight of his arm, and had but an inch to spare. He thrust again at the throat, and the unicorn parried the sword-thrust almost contemptuously. Again and again the unicorn aimed fair at Orion's heart; the huge white beast stepped forward pressing Orion back. That graceful bowing neck, with its white arch of hard muscle driving the deadly horn, was wearying Orion's arm. Once more he thrust and failed; he saw the unicorn's eye flash wickedly in the starlight, he saw all white before him the fearful arch of its neck, he knew he could turn aside its heavy blows no more; and then a hound got a grip in front of the right shoulder. No moments passed before many another hound leaped on to the unicorn, each with a chosen grip, for all that they looked like a rabble rolling and heaving by chance. Orion thrust no more, for many hounds all at once were between him and his enemy's throat. Awful groans came from the unicorn, such sounds as are not heard in the fields we know; and then there was no sound but the deep growl of the hounds that roared over the wonderful carcase as they wallowed in fabulous blood.

Chapter XX

A Historical Fact

Amongst the weary hounds refreshed with fury and triumph, Orion stepped with his whip and drove them away from the monstrous dead body, and sent the lash quivering round in a wide circle, while in his other hand he took his sword and cut off the unicorn's head. He also took the skin of the long white neck and brought it away dangling empty from the head. All the while the hounds bayed and made eager rushes one by one at that magical carcase whenever one saw a chance of eluding the whip; so that it was long before Orion got his trophy, for he had to work as hard with his whip as with his sword. But at last he had it slung by a leather thong over his shoulders, the great horn pointing upwards past the right side of his head, and the smeared skin hanging down along his back. And while he arranged it thus he allowed his hounds to worry the body again and taste that wonderful blood. Then he called to them and blew a note on his horn and turned slowly home towards Erl, and they all followed behind him. And the two foxes stole up to taste the curious blood, for they had sat and waited for this.

While the unicorn was climbing his last hill Orion felt such fatigue that he could have gone little further, but now that the heavy head hung from his shoulders all his fatigue was gone and he trod with a lightness such as he had in the mornings, for it was his first unicorn. And his hounds seemed refreshed as though the blood they had lapped had some strange power in it, and they came home riotously, gambolling and rushing ahead as when newly loosed from their kennels.

Thus Orion came home over the downs in the night, till he saw the valley before him full of the smoke of Erl, where one late light was burning in a window of one of his towers. And, coming down the slopes by familiar ways, he brought his hounds to their kennels; and just before dawn had touched the heights of the downs he blew his horn before his postern door. And the aged guardian of the door when he opened it to Orion saw the great horn of the unicorn bobbing over his head.

This was the horn that was sent in later years as a gift from the Pope to King Francis. Benvenuto Cellini tells of it in his memoirs. He tells how Pope Clement sent for him and a certain Tobbia, and ordered them to make designs for the setting of a unicorn's horn, the finest ever seen. Judge then of Orion's delight when the horn of the first unicorn he ever took was such as to be esteemed generations later the finest ever seen, and in no less a city than Rome, with all her opportunities to acquire and compare such things. For a number of these curious horns must have been available for the Pope to have selected for the gift the finest ever seen; but in the simpler days of my story the rarity of the horn was so great that unicorns were still considered fabulous. The year of the gift to King Francis would be about 1530, the horn being mounted in gold; and the contract went to Tobbia and not to Benvenuto Cellini. I mention the date because there are those who care little for a tale if it be not here and there supported by history, and who even in history care more for fact than philosophy. If any such reader have followed the fortunes of Orion so far he will be hungry by now for a date or a historical fact. As for the date, I give him 1530. While for the historical fact I select that generous gift recorded by Benvenuto Cellini, because it may well be that just where he came to unicorns such a reader may have felt furthest away from history and have felt loneliest just at this point for want of historical things. How the unicorn's horn found its way from the Castle of Erl, and in what hands it wandered, and how it came at last to the City of Rome, would of course make another book.

But all that I need say now about that horn is that Orion took the whole head to Threl, who took off the skin and washed it and boiled the skull for hours, and replaced the skin and stuffed the neck with straw; and Orion set it in the midmost place among all the heads that hung in the high hall. And the rumour went all through Erl, as swift as unicorns gallop, telling of this fine horn that Orion had won. So that the parliament of Erl met again in the forge of Narl. They sat at the table there debating the rumour; and others besides Threl had seen the head. And at first, for the sake of old divisions, some held to their opinion that there had been no unicorn. They drank Narl's goodly mead and argued against the monster. But after a while, whether Threl's argument convinced them, or whether as is more likely, they yielded from generosity, which arose like a beautiful flower out of the mellow mead, whatever it was the debate of those that opposed the unicorn languished, and when the vote was put it was declared that Orion had killed a unicorn, which he had hunted hither from beyond the fields we know.

And at this they all rejoiced; for they saw at last the magic for which they had longed, and for which they had planned so many years ago, when all were younger and had had more hope in their plans. And as soon as the vote was taken Narl brought out more mead, and they drank again to mark the happy occasion: for magic at last, said they, had come on Orion, and a glorious future surely awaited Erl. And the long room and the candles and the friendly men and the deep comfort of mead made it easy to look a little way forward into time and to see a year or so that had not yet come, and to see coming glories glowing a little way off. And they told again of the days, but nearer now, when the distant lands should hear of the vale they loved: they told again of the fame of the fields of Erl going from city to city. One praised its castle, another its huge high downs, another the vale itself all hidden from every land, another the dear quaint houses built by an olden folk, another the deep of the woods that lay over the sky-line; and all spoke of the time when the wide world should hear of it all, because of the magic that there was in Orion; for they knew that the world has a quick ear for magic, and always turns toward the wonderful even though it be nearly asleep. Their voices were high, praising magic, telling again of the unicorn, glorying in the future of Erl, when suddenly in the doorway stood the Freer. He was there in his long white robe with its trimming of mauve, in the door with the night behind him. As they looked, in the light of their candles, they could see he was wearing an emblem, on a chain of gold round his neck. Narl bade him welcome, some moved a chair to the table; but he had heard them speak of the unicorn. He lifted his voice from where he stood, and addressed them. "Cursed be unicorns," he said, "and all their ways, and all things that be magic."

In the awe that suddenly changed the mellow room one cried: "Master! Curse not us!"

"Good Freer," said Narl, "we hunted no unicorn."

But the Freer raised up his hand against unicorns and cursed them yet. "Curst be their horn," he cried, "and the place where they dwell, and the lilies whereon they feed, curst be all songs that tell of them. Curst be they utterly with everything that dwelleth beyond salvation."

He paused to allow them to renounce the unicorns, standing still in the doorway, looking sternly into the room.

And they thought of the sleekness of the unicorn's hide, his swiftness, the grace of his neck, and his dim beauty cantering by when he came past Erl in the evening. They thought of his stalwart and redoubtable horn; they remembered old songs that told of him. They sat in uneasy silence and would not renounce the unicorn.

And the Freer knew what they thought and he raised his hand again, clear in the candle-light with the night behind him. "Curst be their speed," he said, "and their sleek white hide; curst be their beauty and all that they have of magic, and everything that walks by enchanted streams."

And still he saw in their eyes a lingering love for those things that he forbade, and therefore he ceased not yet. He lifted his voice yet louder and continued, with his eye sternly upon those troubled faces: "And curst be trolls, elves, goblins and fairies upon the Earth, and hypogriffs and Pegasus in the air, and all the tribes of the mer-folk under the sea. Our holy rites forbid them. And curst be all doubts, all singular dreams, all fancies. And from magic may all true folk be turned away. Amen."

He turned round suddenly and was into the night. A wind loitered about the door, then flapped it to. And the large room in the forge of

Narl was as it had been but a few moments before, yet the mellow mood of it seemed dulled and dim. And then Narl spoke, rising up at the table's end and breaking the gloom of the silence. "Did we plan our plans," he said, "so long ago, and put our faith in magic, that we should now renounce magical things and curse our neighbours, the harmless folk beyond the fields we know, and the beautiful things of the air, and dead mariners' lovers dwelling beneath the sea?"

"No, no," said some. And they quaffed their mead again.

And then one rose with his horn of mead held high, then another and then another, till all were standing upright all round the light of the candles. "Magic!" one cried. And the rest with one accord took up his cry till all were shouting "Magic."

The Freer on his homeward way heard that cry of Magic, he gathered his sacred robe more closely around him and clutched his holy things, and said a spell that kept him from sudden demons and the doubtful things of the mist.

Chapter XXI

On the Verge of Earth

And on that day Orion rested his hounds. But the next day he rose early and went to his kennels and loosened the joyous hounds in the shining morning, and led them out of the valley and over the downs towards the frontier of twilight again. And he took his bow with him no more, but only his sword and his whip; for he had come to love the joy of his fifteen hounds when they hunted the one-horned monster, and felt that he shared the joy of every hound; while to shoot one with an arrow would be but a single joy.

All day he went over the fields, greeting some farmer here and there, or worker in the field, and gaining greetings in return, and good wishes for sport. But when evening came and he was near the frontier, fewer and fewer greeted him as he passed, for he was manifestly travelling where none went, whence even their thoughts held back. So he went lonely, yet cheered by his eager thoughts, and happy in the comradeship of his hounds; and both his thoughts and his hounds were all for the chase.

And so he came to the barrier of twilight again, where the hedges ran down to it from the fields of men and turned strange and dim in a glow that is not of our Earth and disappeared in the twilight. He stood with his hounds close in against one of these hedges just where it touched the barrier. The light just there on the hedge, if like anything of our Earth, was like the misty dimness that flashes upon a hedge, seen only across one field, when touched by the rainbow: in the sky the rainbow is clear, but close across one wide field the rainbow's end scarcely shows, yet a heavenly strangeness has touched and altered the hedge. In some such light as that glowed the last of the hawthorns that grew in the fields of men. And just beyond it, like a liquid opal, all full of wandering lights, lay the barrier through which no man can see, and no sound come but the sound of the elfin horns, and only that to the ears of very few. The horns were blowing now, piercing that barrier of dim light and silence with the magical resonance of their silver note, that seemed to beat past all things intervening to come to Orion's ear, as the sunlight beats through ether to illumine the vales of the moon.

The horns died down, and nothing whispered from Elfland; and all the sounds thenceforth were the sounds of an earthly evening. Even these grew few, and still no unicorns came.

A dog barked far away: a cart, the sole sound on an empty road, went homeward wearily: someone spoke in a lane, and then left the silence unbroken, for words seemed to offend the hush that was over all our fields. And in the hush Orion gazed at the frontier, watching for the unicorns that never came, expecting each moment to see one step through the twilight. But he had done unwisely in coming to the same spot at which he had found the five unicorns only two days before. For of all creatures the unicorns are the wariest, guarding their beauty from the eye of man with never ceasing watchfulness; dwelling all day beyond the fields we know, and only entering them rarely at evening, when all is still, and with the utmost vigilance, and venturing even then scarcely beyond the edges. To come on such animals twice at the same spot within two days with hounds, after hunting and killing one of them, was more unlikely than Orion thought. But his heart was full of the triumph of his hunt, and the scene of it lured him back to it in the way that such scenes have. And now he gazed at the frontier, waiting for one of these great creatures to come proudly through, a great tangible shape out of the dim opalescence. And no unicorn came.

And standing gazing there so long, that curious boundary began to lure him till his thoughts went roaming with its wandering lights and he desired the peaks of Elfland. And well they knew that lure who dwelt on those farms lying all along the edge of the fields we know, and wisely kept their eyes turned ever away from that wonder that lay with its marvel of colours so near to the backs of their houses. For there was a beauty in it such as is not in all our fields; and it is told those farmers in youth how, if they gaze upon those wandering lights, there will remain no joy for them in the goodly fields, the fine, brown furrows or the waves of wheat, or in any things of ours; but their hearts will be far from here with elfin things, yearning always for unknown mountains and for folk not blessed by the Freer.

And standing now, while our earthly evening waned, upon the very edge of that magical twilight, the things of Earth rushed swiftly from his remembrance, and suddenly all his care was for elfin things. Of all the folk that trod the paths of men he remembered only his mother, and suddenly knew, as though the twilight had told him, that she was enchanted and he of a magical line. And none had told him this, but he knew it now.

For years he had wondered through many an evening and guessed where his mother was gone: he had guessed in lonely silence; none knew what the child was guessing: and now an answer seemed to hang in the air; it seemed as though she were only a little way off across the enchanted twilight that divided those farms from Elfland. He moved three steps and came to the frontier itself; his foot was the furthest that stood in the fields we know: against his face the frontier lay like a mist, in which all the colours of pearls were dancing gravely. A hound stirred as he moved, the pack turned their heads and eyed him; he stood, and they rested again. He tried to see through the barrier, but saw nothing but wandering lights that were made by the massing of twilights from the ending of thousands of days, which had been preserved by magic to build that barrier there. Then he called to his mother across that mighty gap, those few preserved by magic to build that barrier there. Then he upon one side Earth and the haunts of men, and the time that we measure by minutes and hours and years, and upon the other Elfland and another way of time. He called to her twice and listened, and called again; and never a cry or a whisper came out of Elfland. He felt then the magnitude of the gulf that divided him from her, and knew it to be vast and dark and strong, like the gulfs that set apart our times from a bygone day, or that stand between daily life and the things of dream, or between folk tilling the Earth and the heroes of song, or between those living yet and those they mourn. And the barrier twinkled and sparkled as though so airy a thing never divided lost years from that fleeing hour called Now.

He stood there with the cries of Earth faint in the late evening, behind him, and the mellow glow of the soft earthly twilight; and before him, close to his face, the utter silence of Elfland, and the barrier that made that silence, gleaming with its strange beauty. And now he thought no more of earthly things, but only gazed into that wall of twilight, as prophets tampering with forbidden lore gaze into cloudy crystals. And to all that was elvish in Orion's blood, to all that he had of magic from his mother, the little lights of the twilight-builded boundary lured and tempted and beckoned. He thought of his mother dwelling in lonely ease beyond the rage of Time, he thought of the glories of Elfland, dimly known by magical memories that he had had from his mother. The little cries of the earthly evening behind him he heeded no more nor heard. And with all these little cries were lost to him also the ways and the needs of men, the things they plan, the things they toil for and hope for, and all the little things their patience achieves. In the new knowledge that had come to him beside this

glittering boundary that he was of magical blood he desired at once to
cast off his allegiance to Time, and to leave the lands that lay under
Time's dominion and were ever scourged by his tyranny, to leave them
with no more than five short paces, and to enter the ageless land where
his mother sat with her father while he reigned on his misty throne in
that hall of bewildering beauty at which only song has guessed. No
more was Erl his home, no more were the ways of man his ways: their
fields to his feet no more! But the peaks of the Elfin Mountains were to
him now what welcoming eaves of straw are to earthly labourers at
evening; the fabulous, the unearthly, were to Orion home. Thus had
that barrier of twilight, too long seen, enchanted him; so much more
magical was it than any earthly evening.

And there are those that might have gazed long at it and even yet
turned away; but not easily Orion; for though magic has power to
charm worldly things they respond to enchantment heavily and slowly,
while all that was magic in Orion's blood flashed answer to the magic
that shown in the rampart of Elfland. It was made of the rarest lights
that wander in air, and the fairest flashes of sunlight that astonish our
fields through storm, and the mists of little streams, and the glow of
flowers in moonlight, and all the ends of our rainbows with all their
beauty and magic, and scraps of the gloaming of evenings long
treasured in aged minds. Into this enchantment he stepped to have done
with mundane things; but as his foot touched the twilight a hound that
had sat behind him under the hedge, held back from the chase so long,
stretched its body a little and uttered one of those low cries of
impatience that amongst the ways of man most nearly resembles a
yawn. And old habit, at that sound made Orion turn his head, and he
saw the hound and went up to him for a moment, and patted him and
would have said farewell; but all the hounds were around him then,
nosing his hands and looking up at his face. And standing there
amongst his eager hounds, Orion, who but a moment before was
dreaming of fabulous things with thoughts that floated over the magical
lands and scaled the enchanted peaks of the Elfin Mountains, was
suddenly at the call of his earthly lineage. It was not that he cared more
to hunt than to be with his mother beyond the fret of time, in the lands
of her father lovelier than anything song hath said; it was not that he
loved his hounds so much that he could not leave them; but his fathers
had followed the chase age after age, as his mother's line had
timelessly followed magic; and the call towards magic was strong
while he looked on magical things, and the old earthly line was as
strong to beckon him to the chase. The beautiful boundary of twilight
had drawn his desires towards Elfland, next moment his hounds had
turned him another way: it is hard for any of us to avoid the grip of
external things.

For some moments Orion stood thinking among his hounds, trying to decide which way to turn, trying to weigh the easy lazy ages, that hung over untroubled lawns and the listless glories of Elfland, with the good brown plough and the pasture and the little hedges of Earth. But the hounds were around him, nosing, crying, looking into his eyes, speaking to him if tails and paws and large brown eyes can speak, saying "Away! Away!" To think amongst all that tumult was impossible; he could not decide, and the hounds had it their way, and he and they went, together, home over the fields we know.

Chapter XXII

Orion Appoints a Whip

And many times again, while the winter wore away, Orion went back again with his hounds to that wonderful boundary, and waited there while the earthly twilight faded; and sometimes saw the unicorns come through, craftily, silently, when our fields were still, great beautiful shapes of white. But he brought back no more horns to the castle of Erl, nor hunted again across the fields we know; for the unicorns when they came moved into our fields no more than a few bare paces, and Orion was not able to cut one off again. Once when he tried he nearly lost all his hounds, some being already within the boundary when he beat them back with his whip; another two yards and the sound of his earthly horn could never more have reached them. It was this that taught him that for all the power that he had over his hounds, and even though in that power was something of magic, yet one man without help could not hunt hounds, so near to that edge over which if one should stray it would be lost forever.

After this Orion watched the lads at their games in evenings at Erl, till he had marked three that in speed and strength seemed to excel the rest; and two of these he chose to be whippers-in. He went to the cottage of one of them when the games were over, just as the lights were lit, a tall lad with great speed of limb; the lad and his mother were there and both rose from the table as the father opened the door and Orion came in. And cheerily Orion asked the lad if he would come with the hounds and carry a whip and prevent any from straying. And a silence fell. All knew that Orion hunted strange beasts and took his hounds to strange places. None there had ever stepped beyond the fields we know. The lad feared to pass beyond them. His parents were full loth to let him go. At length the silence was broken by excuses and muttered sentences and unfinished things, and Orion saw that the lad would not come.

He went then to the house of the other. There too the candles were lit and a table spread. There were two old women there and the lad at their supper. And to them Orion told how he needed a whipper-in, and asked the lad to come. Their fear in that house was more marked. The old women cried out together that the lad was too young, that he could not run so well as he used to, that he was not worthy of so great an honour, that dogs never would trust him. And much more than this they said, till they became incoherent. Orion left them and went to the house of the third. It was the same here. The elders had desired magic for Erl, but the actual touch of it, or the mere thought of it, perturbed the folk in their cottages. None would spare their sons to go whither they knew not, to have dealings with things that rumour, like a large and sinister shadow, had so grimly magnified in the hamlet of Erl. So Orion went alone with his hounds when he took them up from the valley and went eastwards over our fields where Earth's folk would not go.

It was late in the month of March, and Orion slept in his tower, when there came up to him from far below, shrill and clear in the early morning, the sound of his peacocks calling. The bleat of sheep far up on the downs came to wake him too, and cocks were crowing clamourously, for Spring was singing through the sunny air. He rose and went to his hounds; and soon early labourers saw him go up the steep side of the valley with all his hounds behind him, tan patches against the green. And so he passed over the fields we know. And so he was come, before the sun had set, to that strip of land from which all men turned away, where westward stood men's houses among fields of fat brown clay and eastward the Elfin Mountains shone over the boundary of twilight.

He went with his hounds along the last hedge, down to the boundary. And no sooner had he come there than he saw a fox quite close slip out of the twilight between Earth and Elfland, and run a few yards along the edge of our fields and then slip back again. And of this Orion thought nothing, for it is the way of the fox thus to haunt the edge of Elfland and to return again to our fields: it is thus that he brings us something of which none of our cities guess. But soon the fox appeared again out of the twilight and ran a little way and was back in the luminous barrier once more. Then Orion watched to see what the fox was doing. And yet again it appeared in the field we know, and dodged back into the twilight. And the hounds watched too, and showed no longing to hunt it, for they had tasted fabulous blood.

Orion walked along beside the twilight in the direction in which the fox was going, with his curiosity growing the more that the fox dodged in and out of our fields. The hounds followed him slowly and soon lost their interest in what the fox was doing. And all at once the curious thing was explained, for Lurulu all of a sudden skipped through the twilight, and that troll appeared in our fields: it was with him that the fox was playing.

"A man," said Lurulu aloud to himself, or to his comrade the fox, speaking in troll-talk. And all at once Orion remembered the troll that had come into his nursery with his little charm against time, and had leaped from shelf to shelf and across the ceiling and enraged Ziroonderel who had feared for her crockery.

"The troll!" he said, also in troll-talk; for his mother had murmured it to him as a child when she told him tales of the trolls and their age-old songs.

"Who is this that knows troll-talk?" said Lurulu.

And Orion told his name, and this meant nothing to Lurulu. But he squatted down and rummaged a little while in what answers in trolls to our memory; and during his ransacking of much trivial remembrance that had eluded the destruction of time in the fields we know, and the listless apathy of unchanging ages in Elfland, he came all at once on his remembrance of Erl; and looked at Orion again and began to cogitate. And at this same moment Orion told to the troll the august name of his mother. At once Lurulu made what is known amongst the trolls of Elfland as the abasement of the five points; that is to say he bowed himself to the ground on his two knees, his two hands and his forehead. Then he sprang up again with a high leap into the air; for reverence rested not on his spirit long.

"What are you doing in men's fields?" said Orion.

"Playing" said Lurulu.

"What do you do in Elfland?"

"Watch time," said Lurulu.

"That would not amuse me," said Orion.

"You've never done it," said Lurulu. "You cannot watch time in the fields of men."

"Why not?" asked Orion.

"It moves too fast."

Orion pondered awhile on this but could make nothing of it; because, never having gone from the fields we know, he knew only one pace of time, and so had no means of comparison.

"How many years have gone over you," asked the troll, "since we spoke in Erl?"

"Years?" said Orion.

"A hundred?" guessed the troll.

"Nearly twelve," said Orion. "And you?"

"It is still to-day" said the troll.

And Orion would not speak any more of time, for he cared not for the discussion of a subject of which he appeared to know less than a common troll.

"Will you carry a whip," he said, "and run with my hounds when we hunt the unicorn over the fields we know."

Lurulu looked searchingly at the hounds, watching their brown eyes: the hounds turned doubtful noses towards the troll and sniffed enquiringly.

"They are dogs," said the troll, as though that were against them. "Yet they have pleasant thoughts."

"You will carry the whip then," said Orion.

"M, yes. Yes," said the troll.

So Orion gave him his own whip there and then, and blew his horn and went away from the twilight, and told Lurulu to keep the hounds together and to bring them on behind him.

And the hounds were uneasy at the sight of the troll, and sniffed and sniffed again, but could not make him human, and were loth to obey a creature no larger than them. They ran up to him through curiosity, and ran away in disgust, and straggled through disobedience. But the boundless resources of that nimble troll were not thus easily thwarted, and the whip went suddenly up, looking three times as large in that tiny hand, and the lash flew forward and cracked on the tip of a hound's nose. The hound yelped, then looked astonished, and the rest were uneasy still: they must have thought it an accident. But again the lash shot forward and cracked on another nose-tip; and the hounds saw then that it was not chance that guided those stinging shots, but a deadly unerring eye. And from that time on they reverenced Lurulu, although he never smelt human.

So went Orion and his pack of hounds in the late evening homewards, and no sheep-dog kept the flock on wolf-haunted wold safer or closer than Lurulu kept the pack: he was on each flank or behind them, wherever a straggler was, and could leap right over the pack from side to side. And the pale-blue Elfin Mountains faded from view before Orion had gone from the frontier as much as a hundred paces, for their gloomless peaks were hid by the earthly darkness that was deepening wide over the fields we know.

Homeward they went, and soon there appeared above them the wandering multitude of our earth-seen stars. Lurulu now and then looked up to marvel at them, as we have all done at some time; but for the most part he fixed his attention on the hounds, for now that he was in earthly fields he was concerned with the things of Earth. And never one hound loitered but that Lurulu's whip would touch him, with its tiny explosion, perhaps on the tip of its tail, scattering a little dust of fragments of hair and whipcord; and the hound would yelp and run in to the others, and all the pack would know that another of those unerring shots had gone home.

A certain grace with a whip, a certain sureness of aim, comes when a life is devoted to the carrying of a whip amongst hounds; comes, say, in twenty years. And sometimes it runs in families; and that is better than years of practice. But neither years of practice nor the wont of the whip in the blood can give the certain aim that one thing can; and that one thing is magic. The hurl of the lash, as immediate as the sudden turn of an eye, its flash to a chosen spot as direct as sight, were not of this Earth. And though the cracks of that whip might have seemed to passing men to be no more than the work of an earthly huntsman, yet not a hound but knew that there was in it more than this, a thing from beyond our fields.

There was a touch of dawn in the sky when Orion saw again the village of Erl, sending up pillars of smoke from early fires below him, and came with his hounds and his new whipper-in down the side of the valley. Early windows winked at him as he went down the street and came in the silence and chill to the empty kennels. And when the hounds were all curled up on their straw he found a place for Lurulu, a mouldering loft in which were sacks and a few heaps of hay: from a pigeon-loft just beyond it some of the pigeons had strayed, and dwelt all along the rafters. There Orion left Lurulu, and went to his tower, cold with the want of sleep and food; and weary as he would not have been if he had found a unicorn, but the noise of the troll's chatter when he had found him on the frontier had made it useless to watch for those wary beasts that evening. Orion slept. But the troll in the mouldering loft sat long on his bundle of hay observing the ways of time. He saw through cracks in old shutters the stars go moving by; he saw them pale: he saw the other light spread; he saw the wonder of sunrise: he felt the gloom of the loft all full of the coo of the pigeons; he watched their restless ways: he heard wild birds stir in near elms, and men abroad in the morning, and horses and carts and cows; and everything changing as the morning grew. A land of change! The decay of the boards in the loft, and the moss outside in the mortar, and old lumber mouldering away, all seemed to tell the same story. Change and nothing abiding. He thought of the age-old calm that held the beauty of Elfland. And then he thought of the tribe of trolls he had left, wondering what they would think of the ways of Earth. And the pigeons were suddenly terrified by wild peals of Lurulu's laughter.

Chapter XXIII

Lurulu Watches the Restlessness of Earth

As the day wore on and still Orion slept heavily, and even the hounds lay silent in their kennels a little way off, and the coming and going of men and carts below had nothing to do with the troll, Lurulu began to feel lonely. So thick are the brown trolls in the dells they inhabit that none feels lonely there. They sit there silent, enjoying the beauty of Elfland or their own impudent thoughts, or at rare moments when Elfland is stirred from its deep natural calm their laughter floods the dells. They were no more lonely there than rabbits are. But in all the fields of Earth there was only one troll; and that troll felt lonely. The door of the pigeon loft was open some ten feet from the door of the hayloft, and some six feet higher. A ladder led to the hayloft, clamped to the wall with iron; but nothing at all communicated with the pigeon-loft lest cats should go that way. From it came the murmur of abundant life, which attracted the lonely troll. The jump from door to door was nothing to him, and he landed in the pigeon-loft in his usual attitude, with a look of impudent welcome upon his face. But the pigeons poured away on a roar of wings through their windows, and the troll was still lonely.

He liked the pigeon-loft as soon as he looked at it. He liked the signs that he saw of teeming life, the hundred little houses of slate and plaster, the myriad feathers, and the musty smell. He liked the age-old ease of the sleepy loft, and the huge spiders-webs that draped the corners, holding years and years of dust. He did not know what cobwebs were, never having seen them in Elfland, but he admired their workmanship.

The age of the pigeon-loft that had filled the corners with cobwebs, and broken patches of plaster away from the wall, shewing ruddy bricks beneath, and laid bare the laths in the roof and even the slates beyond, gave to the dreamy place an air not unlike to the calm of Elfland; but below it and all around Lurulu noted the restlessness of Earth. Even the sunlight through the little ventilation-holes that shone on the wall moved.

Presently there came the roar of the pigeons' returning wings and the crash of their feet on the slate roof above him, but they did not yet come in again to their homes. He saw the shadow of this roof cast on another roof below him, and the restless shadows of the pigeons along the edge. He observed the grey lichen covering most of the lower roof, and the neat round patches of newer yellow lichen on the shapeless mass of the grey. He heard a duck call out slowly six or seven times. He heard a man come into a stable below him and lead a horse away. A hound woke and cried out. Some jackdaws, disturbed from some tower, passed over high in the air with boisterous voices. He saw big clouds go hurrying along the tops of far hills. He heard a wild pigeon call from a neighbouring tree. Some men went by talking. And after a while he perceived to his astonishment what he had had no leisure to notice on his previous visit to Erl, that even the shadows of houses moved; for he saw that the shadow of the roof under which he sat had moved a little on the roof below, over the grey and yellow lichen. Perpetual movement and perpetual change! He contrasted it, in wonder, with the deep calm of his home, where the moment moved more slowly than the shadows of houses here, and did not pass until all the content with which a moment is stored had been drawn from it by every creature in Elfland.

And then with a whirring and whining of wings the pigeons began to come back. They came from the tops of the battlements of the highest tower of Erl, on which they had sheltered awhile, feeling guarded by its great height and its hoary age from this strange new thing that they feared. They came back and sat on the sills of their little windows and looked in with one eye at the troll. Some were all white, but the grey ones had rainbow-coloured necks that were scarce less lovely than those colours that made the splendour of Elfland; and Lurulu as they watched him suspiciously where he sat still in a corner longed for their dainty companionship. And, when these restless children of a restless air and Earth still would not enter, he tried to soothe them with the restlessness to which they were accustomed and in which he believed all folk that dwelt in our fields delighted. He leaped up suddenly; he sprang on to a slate-built house for a pigeon high on a wall; he darted across to the next wall and back to the floor; but there was an outcry of wings and the pigeons were gone. And gradually he learned that the pigeons preferred stillness.

Their wings roared back soon to the roof; their feet thumped and clicked on the slates again; but not for long did they return to their homes. And the lonely troll looked out of their windows observing the ways of Earth. He saw a water-wagtail light on the roof below him: he watched it until it went. And then two sparrows came to some corn that had been dropped on the ground: he noted them too. Each was an entirely new genus to the troll, and he showed no more interest as he watched every movement of the sparrows than should we if we met with an utterly unknown bird. When the sparrows were gone the duck quacked again, so deliberately that another ten minutes passed while Lurulu tried to interpret what it was saying, and although he desisted then because other interests attracted him he felt sure it was something important. Then the jackdaws tumbled by again, but their voices sounded frivolous, and Lurulu did not give them much attention. To the pigeons on the roof that would not come home he listened long, not trying to interpret what they were saying, yet satisfied with the case as the pigeons put it; feeling that they told the story of life, and that all was well. And he felt as he listened to the low talk of the pigeons that Earth must have been going on for a long time.

Beyond the roofs the tall trees rose up, leafless except for evergreen oaks and some laurels and pines and yews, and the ivy that climbed up trunks, but the buds of the beech were getting ready to burst: and the sunlight glittered and flashed on the buds and leaves, and the ivy and laurel shone. A breeze passed by and some smoke drifted from some near chimney. Far away Lurulu saw a huge grey wall of stone that circled a garden all asleep in the sun; and clear in the sunlight he saw a butterfly sail by, and swoop when it came to the garden. And then he saw two peacocks go slowly past. He saw the shadow of the roofs darkening the lower part of the shining trees. He heard a cock crow somewhere, and a hound spoke out again. And then a sudden

Pigeons? sparrows, ducks???

shower rained on the roofs, and at once the pigeons wanted to come home. They alighted outside their little windows again and all looked sideways at the troll; Lurulu kept very still this time; and after a while the pigeons, though they saw that he was by no means one of themselves, agreed that he did not belong to the tribe of cat, and returned at last to the street of their tiny houses and there continued their curious age-old tale. And Lurulu longed to repay them with curious tales of the trolls, the treasured legends of Elfland, but found that he could not make them understand troll-talk. So he sat and listened to them talking, till it seemed to him they were trying to lull the restlessness of Earth, and thought that they might by drowsy incantation be putting some spell against time, through which it could not come to harm their nests; for the power of time was not made clear to him yet and he knew not yet that nothing in our fields has the strength to hold out against time. The very nests of the pigeons were built on the ruins of old nests, on a solid layer of crumbled things that time had made in that pigeon-loft, as outside it the strata are made from the ruins of hills. So vast and ceaseless a ruin was not yet clear to the troll, for his sharp understanding had only been meant to guide him through the lull and the calm of Elfland, and he busied himself with a tinier consideration. For seeing that the pigeons seemed now amicable he leapt back to his hayloft and returned with a bundle of hay, which he put down in a corner to make himself comfortable there. When the pigeons saw all this movement they looked at him sideways again, jerking their necks queerly, but in the end decided to accept the troll as a lodger; and he curled up on his hay and listened to the history of Earth, which he believed the tale of the pigeons to be, though he did not know their language.

But the day wore on and hunger came on the troll, far sooner than ever it did in Elfland, where even when he was hungry he had no more to do than to reach up and take the berries that hung low from the trees, that grew in the forest that bordered the dells of the trolls. And it is because the trolls eat them whenever hunger comes on them, which it rarely does, that these curious fruits are called trollberries. He leaped now from the pigeon-loft and scampered abroad, looking all round for trollberries. And there were no berries at all, for there is but one season for berries, as we know well; it is one of the tricks of time. But that all the berries on Earth should pass away for a period was to the troll too astounding to be comprehended at all. He was all among farm-buildings, and presently he saw a rat humping himself slowly along through a dark shed. He knew nothing of rat-talk; but it is a curious thing that when any two folk are after the same thing, each somehow knows what the other is after, at once, as soon as he sees him. We are all partially blind to other folks' occupations, but when we meet anyone engaged in our own pursuit then somehow we soon seem to know without being told. And the moment that Lurulu saw the rat in the shed he seemed to know that it was looking for food. So he followed the rat quietly. And soon the rat came up to a sack of oats, and to open that took him no longer than it does to shell a row of peas, and soon he was eating the oats.

"Are they good?" said the troll in troll-talk.

The rat looked at him dubiously, noting his resemblance to man, and on the other hand his unlikeness to dogs. But on the whole the rat was dissatisfied, and after a long look turned away in silence and went out of the shed. Then Lurulu ate the oats and found they were good.

When he had had enough oats the troll returned to the pigeon-loft, and sat a long while there at one of the little windows looking out across the roofs at the strange new ways of time. And the shadow upon the trees went higher, and the glitter was gone from the laurels and all the lower leaves. And then the light of the ivy-leaves and the holm-oaks turned from silvery to pale gold. And the shadow went higher still. All the world full of change.

An old man with a narrow long white beard came slowly to the kennels, and opened the door and went in and fed the hounds with meat that he brought from a shed. All the evening rang with the hounds' outcry. And presently the old man came out again, and his slow departure seemed to the watchful troll yet more of the restlessness of Earth.

And then a man came slowly leading a horse to the stable below the pigeon-loft; and went away again and left the horse eating. The shadows were higher now on walls and roofs and trees. Only the tree-tops and the tip of a high belfry had the light any longer. The ruddy buds on high beeches were glowing now like dull rubies. And a great serenity came in the pale blue sky, and small clouds leisurely floating there turned to a flaming orange, past which the rooks went homewards to some clump of trees under the downs. It was a peaceful scene. And yet to the troll, as he watched in the musty loft amongst generations of feathers, the noise of the rooks and their multitude thronging the sky, the dull continual sound of the horse eating, the leisurely sound now and then of homeward feet, and the slow shutting of gates, seemed to be proof that nothing ever rested in all the fields we know; and the sleepy lazy village that dreamed in the Vale of Erl, and that knew no more of other lands than their folk knew of its story, seemed to that simple troll to be a vortex of restlessness.

And now the sunlight was gone from the highest places, and a moon a few days old was shining over the pigeon-loft, out of sight of Lurulu's window, but filling the air with a strange new tint. And all these changes bewildered him, so that he thought awhile of returning to Elfland, but the whim came again to his mind to astonish the other trolls; and while this whim was on him he slipped down from the loft, and went to find Orion.

Chapter XXIV

Lurulu Speaks of Earth and the Ways of Men

The troll had found Orion in his castle and had laid his plan before
him. Briefly the plan was to have more whips for the pack. For one
alone could not always guard every hound from straying when they
went to the boundary of twilight, where but a few yards away lay
spaces from which if a hound ever came home, as lost hounds do at
evening, it would come home all worn and bedraggled with age for its
half hour of straying. Each hound, said Lurulu, should have its troll to
guide it, and to run with it when it hunted, and be its servant when it
came home hungry and muddy. And Orion had seen at once the
unequalled advantage of having each hound controlled by an alert if
tiny intelligence, and had told Lurulu to go for the trolls. So now, while
the hounds were sleeping on boards in a doggy mass in each of their
kennels, for the dogs and the bitches dwelt each in a separate house, the
troll was scurrying over the fields we know through twilight trembling
on the verge of moonlight, with his face turned toward Elfland.

He passed a white farm-house with a little window towards him
that shone bright yellow out of a wall pale blue with a tint that it had
from the moon. Two dogs barked at him and rushed out to chase him,
and this troll would have tricked them and mocked them on any other
day, but now his mind was full to the brim with his mission, and he
heeded them no more than a thistledown would have heeded them on a
windy day of September, and went on bouncing over the tips of the
grasses till the pursuing dogs were far behind and panting.

And long before the stars had paled from any touch of the dawn he
came to the barrier that divides our fields from the home of such things
as him, and leaping forward out of the earthly night, and high through
the barrier of twilight, he arrived on all fours on his natal soil in the
ageless day of Elfland. Through the gorgeous beauty of that heavy air
that outshines our lakes at sunrise, and leaves all our colours pale, he
scampered full of the news he had with which to astonish his kith. He
came to the moors of the trolls where they dwell in their queer
habitations, and uttered the squeaks as he went whereby the trolls
summon their folk; and he came to the forest in which the trolls have
made dwellings in boles of enormous trees; for there be trolls of the
forest and trolls of the moor, two tribes that are friendly and kin; and
there he uttered again the squeaks of the trolls' summons. And soon
there was a rustling of flowers throughout the deeps of the forest, as
though all four winds were blowing, and the rustling grew and grew,
and the trolls appeared, and sat down one by one near Lurulu. And still

the rustling grew, troubling the whole wood, and the brown trolls poured on and sat down round Lurulu. From many a tree-bole, and hollows thick with fern, they came tumbling in; and from the high thin gomaks afar on the moors, to name as are named in Elfland those queer habitations for which there is no earthly name, the odd grey cloth-like material draped tent-wise about a pole. They gathered about him in the dim but glittering light that floated amongst the fronds of those magical trees, whose soaring trunks out-distanced our eldest pines, and shone on the spikes of cacti of which our world little dreams. And when the brown mass of the trolls was all gathered there, till the floor of the forest looked as though an Autumn had come to Elfland, strayed out of the fields we know, and when all the rustling had ceased and the silence was heavy again as it had been for ages, Lurulu spoke to them telling them tales of time.

Never before had such tales been heard in Elfland. Trolls had appeared before in the fields we know, and had come back wondering: but Lurulu amongst the houses of Erl had been in the midst of men; and time, as he told the trolls, moved in the village with more wonderful speed than ever it did in the grass of the fields of Earth. He told how the light moved, he told of shadows, he told how the air was white and bright and pale; he told how for a little while Earth began to grow like Elfland, with a kinder light and the beginning of colours, and then just as one thought of home the light would blink away and the colours be gone. He told of stars. He told of cows and goats and the moon, three horned creatures that he found curious. He had found more wonder in Earth than we remember, though we also saw these things once for the first time; and out of the wonder he felt at the ways of the fields we know, he made many a tale that held the inquisitive trolls and gripped them silent upon the floor of the forest, as though they were indeed a fall of brown leaves in October that a frost had suddenly bound. They heard of chimneys and carts for the first time: with a thrill they heard of windmills. They listened spell-bound to the ways of men; and every now and then, as when he told of hats, there ran through the forest a wave of little yelps of laughter.

Then he said that they should see hats and spades and dog-kennels, and look through casements and get to know the windmill; and a curiosity arose in the forest amongst that brown mass of trolls, for their race is profoundly inquisitive. And Lurulu stopped not here, relying on curiosity alone to draw them from Elfland into the fields we know; but he drew them also with another emotion. For he spoke of the haughty, reserved, high, glittering unicorns, who tarry to speak to trolls no more than cattle when they drink in pools of ours trouble to speak to frogs. They all knew their haunts, they should watch their ways and tell of these things to man, and the outcome of it would be that they should hunt the unicorns with nothing less than dogs. Now however slight their knowledge of dogs, the fear of dogs is—as I have said—universal amongst all creatures that run; and they laughed gustily to think of the unicorns being hunted with dogs. Thus Lurulu lured them toward Earth with spite and curiosity; and knew that he was succeeding; and inwardly chuckled till he was well warmed within. For amongst the trolls none goes in higher repute than one that is able to astound the others, or even to show them any whimsical thing, or to trick or perplex them humorously. Lurulu had Earth to show, whose ways are considered, amongst those able to judge, to be fully as quaint and whimsical as the curious observer could wish.

Then up spake a grizzled troll; one that had crossed too often Earth's border of twilight to watch the ways of men; and, while watching their ways too long, time had grizzled him.

"Shall we go," he said, "from the woods that all folk know, and the pleasant ways of the Land, to see a new thing, and be swept away by time?" And there was a murmur among the trolls, that hummed away through the forest and died out, as on Earth the sound of beetles going home. "Is it not to-day?" he said. "But there they call it to-day, yet none knows what it is: come back through the border again to look at it and it is gone. Time is raging there, like the dogs that stray over our frontier, barking, frightened and angry and wild to be home."

"It is even so," said the trolls, though they did not know; but this was a troll whose words carried weight in the forest. "Let us keep to-day," said that weighty troll, "while we have it, and not be lured where to-day is too easily lost. For every time men lose it their hair grows whiter, their limbs grow weaker and their faces sadder, and they are nearer still to to-morrow."

So gravely he spoke when he uttered that word "to-morrow" that the brown trolls were frightened.

"What happens to-morrow?" one said.

"They die," said the grizzled troll. "And the others dig in their earth and put them in, as I have seen them do, and then they go to Heaven, as I have heard them tell." And a shudder went through the trolls far over the floor of the forest.

And Lurulu who had sat angry all this while to hear that weighty troll speak ill of Earth, where he would have them come, to astonish them with its quaintness, spoke now in defence of Heaven.

"Heaven is a good place," he blurted hotly, though any tales he had heard of it were few.

"All the blessed are there," the grizzled troll replied, "and it is full of angels. What chance would a troll have there? The angels would catch him, for they say on Earth that the angels all have wings; they would catch a troll and smack him forever and ever."

And all the brown trolls in the forest wept.

"We are not so easily caught," Lurulu said.

"They have wings," said the grizzled troll.

And all were sorrowful and shook their heads, for they knew the speed of wings.

The birds of Elfland mostly soared on the heavy air and eyed everlastingly that fabulous beauty which to them was food and nest, and of which they sometimes sang; but trolls playing along the border, peering into the fields we know, had seen the dart and the swoop of earthly birds, wondering at them as we wonder at heavenly things, and knew that if wings were after him a poor troll would scarcely escape. "Welladay," said the trolls.

The grizzled troll said no more, and had no need to, for the forest was full of their sadness as they sat thinking of Heaven and feared that they soon might come there if they dared to inhabit Earth.

And Lurulu argued no more. It was not a time for argument, for the trolls were too sad for reason. So he spoke gravely to them of solemn things, uttering learned words and standing in reverend attitude. Now nothing rejoices the trolls as learning does and solemnity, and they will laugh for hours at a reverend attitude or any semblance of gravity. Thus he won them back again to the levity that is their natural mood. And when this was accomplished he spoke again of Earth, telling whimsical stories of the ways of man.

I do not wish to write the things that Lurulu said of man, lest I should hurt my reader's self-esteem, and thereby injure him or her whom I seek only to entertain; but all the forest rippled and squealed with laughter. And the grizzled troll was able to say no more to check the curiosity which was growing in all that multitude to see who it was that lived in houses and had a hat immediately above him and a chimney higher up, and spoke to dogs and would not speak to pigs, and whose gravity was funnier than anything trolls could do. And the whim was on all those trolls to go at once to Earth, and see pigs and carts and windmills and laugh at man. And Lurulu who had told Orion that he would bring a score of trolls, was hard set to keep the whole brown mass from coming, so quickly change the moods and whims of the trolls: had he let them all have their way there were no trolls left in Elfland, for even the grizzled troll had changed his mind with the rest. Fifty he chose and led them towards Earth's perilous frontier; and away they scurried out of the gloom of the forest, as a whirl of brown oak-leaves scurries on days of November's worst.

Chapter XXV

Lirazel Remembers the Fields We Know

As the trolls scurried earthwards to laugh at the ways of man, Lirazel stirred where she sat on her father's knee, who grave and calm on his throne of mist and ice had hardly moved for twelve of our earthly years. She sighed and the sigh rippled over the fells of dream and lightly troubled Elfland. And the dawns and the sunsets and twilight and the pale blue glow of stars, that are blended together forever to be the light of Elfland, felt a faint touch of sorrow and all their radiance shook. For the magic that caught these lights and the spells that bound them together, to illumine forever the land that owes no allegiance to Time, were not so strong as a sorrow rising dark from a royal mood of a princess of the elvish line. She sighed, for through her long content and across the calm of Elfland there had floated a thought of Earth; so that in the midmost splendours of Elfland, of which song can barely tell, she called to mind common cowslips, and many a trivial weed of the fields we know. And walking in those fields she saw in fancy Orion, upon the other side of the boundary of twilight, remote from her by she knew not what waste of years. And the magical glories of Elfland and its beauty beyond our dreaming, and the deep deep calm in which ages slept, unhurt unhurried by time, and the art of her father that guarded the least of the lilies from fading, and the spells by which he made day-dreams and yearnings true, held her fancy no longer from roving nor contented her any more. And so her sigh blew over the magical land and slightly troubled the flowers.

And her father felt her sorrow and knew that it troubled the flowers and knew that it shook the calm that lay upon Elfland, though no more than a bird would shake a regal curtain, fluttering against its folds, when wandering lost upon a Summer's night. And though he knew too it was but for Earth that she sorrowed, preferring some mundane way to the midmost glories of Elfland, as she sat with him on the throne that may only be told of in song, yet even this moved nothing in his magical heart but compassion; as we might pity a child who in fanes that to us seemed sacred might be found to be sighing for some trivial thing. And the more that Earth seemed to him unworthy of sorrow, being soon come soon gone, the helpless prey of time, an evanescent appearance seen off the coasts of Elfland, too brief for the graver care of a mind weighted with magic, the more he pitied his child for her errant whim that had rashly wandered here, and become entangled—alas—with the things that pass away. Ah, well! she was not content. He felt no wrath against Earth that had lured her fancies away: she was not content with the innermost splendours of Elfland, but she sighed for something more: his tremendous art should give it. So he raised his right arm up from the thing whereon it rested, a part of his mystical throne that was made of music and mirage; he raised his right arm up and a hush fell over Elfland.

The great leaves ceased from their murmur through the green deeps of the forest; silent as carven marble were fabulous bird and monster; and the brown trolls scampering earthwards all halted suddenly hushed. Then out of the hush rose little murmurs of yearning, little sounds as of longing for things that no songs can say, sounds like the voices of tears if each little salt drop could live, and be given a voice to tell of the ways of grief. Then all these little rumours danced gravely into a melody that the master of Elfland called up with his magical hand. And the melody told of dawn coming up over infinite marshes, far away upon Earth or some planet that Elfland did not know; growing slowly out of deep darkness and starlight and bitter cold; powerless, chilly and cheerless, scarce overcoming the stars; obscured by shadows of thunder and hated by all things dark; enduring, growing and glowing; until through the gloom of the marshes and across the chill of the air came all in a glorious moment the splendour of colour; and dawn went onward with this triumphant thing, and the blackest clouds turned slowly rose and rode in a sea of lilac, and the darkest rocks that had guarded night shone now with a golden glow. And when his melody could say no more of this wonder, that had forever been foreign to all the elvish dominions, then the King moved his hand where he held it high, as one might beckon to birds, and called up a dawn over Elfland, luring it from some planet of those that are nearest the sun. And fresh and fair though it came from beyond the bourn of geography, and out of an age long lost and beyond history's ken, a dawn glowed upon Elfland that had known no dawn before. And the dewdrops of Elfland slung from the bended tips of the grasses gathered in that dawn to their tiny spheres and held there shining and wonderful that glory of skies such as ours, the first they had ever seen.

And the dawn grew strangely and slowly over those unwonted lands, pouring upon them the colours that day after day our daffodils, and day after day our wild roses, through all the weeks of their season, drink deep with voluptuous assemblies in utterly silent riot. And a gleam that was new to the forest appeared on the long strange leaves, and shadows unknown to Elfland slipped out from the monstrous tree-boles, and stole over grasses that had not dreamed of their advent; and the spires of that palace perceiving a wonder, less lovely indeed than they, yet knew that the stranger was magic, and uttered an answering gleam from their sacred windows, that flashed over elvish fells like an inspiration and mingled a flush of rose with the blue of the Elfin Mountains. And watchers on wonderful peaks that gazed from their crags for ages, lest from Earth or from any star should come a stranger to Elfland, saw the first blush of the sky as it felt the coming of dawn, and raised their horns and blew that call that warned Elfland against a stranger. And the guardians of savage valleys lifted horns of fabulous bulls and blew the call again in the dark of their awful precipices, and echo carried it on from the monstrous marble faces of rocks that repeated the call to all their barbarous company; so Elfland rang with the warning that a strange thing troubled her coasts. And to the land thus expectant, thus watchful, with magical sabres elate along lonely crags, summoned from blackened scabbards by those horns to repel an enemy, dawn came now wide now golden, the old old wonder we know. And the palace with every marvel and with all its charms and enchantments flashed out of its ice-blue radiance a glory of welcome or rivalry, adding to Elfland a splendour of which only song may say.

It was then that the elfin King moved his hand again, where he held it high by the crystal spires of his crown, and waved a way through the walls of his magical palace, and showed to Lirazel the unmeasured leagues of his kingdom. And she saw by magic, for so long as his fingers made that spell; the dark green forests and all the fells of Elfland, and the solemn pale-blue mountains and the valleys that weird folk guarded, and all the creatures of fable that crept in the dark of huge leaves, and the riotous trolls as they scampered away towards Earth: she saw the watchers lift their horns to their lips, while there flashed a light on the horns that was the proudest triumph of the hidden art of her father, the light of a dawn lured over unthinkable spaces to appease his daughter and comfort her whims and recall her fancies from Earth. She saw the lawns whereon Time had idled for centuries, withering not one bloom of all the boundary of flowers; and the new light coming upon the lawns she loved, through the heavy colour of Elfland, gave them a beauty that they had never known until dawn made this boundless journey to meet the enchanted twilight; and all the while there glowed and flashed and glittered those palace spires of which only song may tell. From that bewildering beauty he turned his eyes away, and looked in his daughter's face to see the wonder with which she would welcome her glorious home as her fancies came back from the fields of age and death, whither—alas—they had wandered. And though her eyes were turned to the Elfin Mountains, whose mystery and whose blue they strangely matched, yet as the Elf King looked in those eyes for which alone he had lured the dawn so far from its natural courses, he saw in their magical deeps a thought of Earth! A thought of Earth, though he had lifted his arm and made a mystical sign with all his might to bring a wonder to Elfland that should content her with home. And all his dominions had exulted in this, and the watchers on awful crags had blown strange calls, and monster and insect and bird and flower had rejoiced with a new joy, and there in the centre of Elfland his daughter thought of Earth.

Had he shown her any wonder but dawn he might have lured home that fancy, but in bringing this exotic beauty to Elfland to blend with its ancient wonders, he awoke memories of morning coming over fields that he knew not, and Lirazel played in fancy in fields once more with Orion, where grew the unenchanted earthly flowers amongst the English grasses.

"Is it not enough?" he said in his strange rich magical voice, and pointed across his wide lands with the fingers that summoned wonder.

She sighed: it was not enough.

And sorrow came upon that enchanted King: he had only his daughter, and she sighed for Earth. There had been once a queen that had reigned with him over Elfland; but she was mortal, and being mortal died. For she would often stray to the hills of Earth to see the may again, or to see the beechwoods in Autumn; and though she stayed but a day when she came to the fields we know, and was back in the palace beyond the twilight before our sun had set, yet Time found her whenever she came; and so she wore away, and soon she died in Elfland; for she was only a mortal. And wondering elves had buried her, as one buries the daughters of men. And now the King was all alone with his daughter, and she had just sighed for Earth. Sorrow was on him, but out of the dark of that sorrow arose, as often with men, and went up singing out of his mourning mind, an inspiration gleaming with laughter and joy. He stood up then and raised up both his arms and his inspiration broke over Elfland in music. And with the tide of that music there went like the strength of the sea an impulse to rise and dance which none in Elfland resisted. Gravely he waved his arms and the music floated from them; and all that stalked through the forest and all that crept upon leaves, all that leaped among craggy heights or browsed upon acres of lilies, all things in all manner of places, yea the sentinel guarding his presence, the lonely mountain-watchers and the trolls as they scampered towards Earth, all danced to a tune that was made of the spirit of Spring, arrived on an earthly morning amongst happy herds of goats.

And the trolls were very near to the frontier now, their faces already puckered to laugh at the ways of men; they were hurrying with all the eagerness of small vain things to be over the twilight that lies between Elfland and Earth: now they went forward no longer, but only glided in circles and intricate spirals, dancing some such dance as the gnats in Summer evenings dance over the fields we know. And grave monsters of fable in deeps of the ferny forest danced minuets that witches had made of their whims and their laughter, long ago long ago in their youth before cities had come to the world. And the trees of the forest heavily lifted slow roots out of the ground and swayed upon them uncouthly and then danced as on monstrous claws, and the insects danced on the huge waving leaves. And in the dark of long caverns weird things in enchanted seclusion rose out of their age-long sleep and danced in the damp.

And beside the wizard King stood, swaying slightly to the rhythm that had set dancing all magical things, the Princess Lirazel with that faint gleam on her face that shone from a hidden smile; for she secretly smiled forever at the power of her great beauty. And all in a sudden moment the Elf King raised one hand higher and held it high and stilled all that danced in Elfland, and gripped by a sudden awe all magical things, and sent over Elfland a melody all made of notes he had caught from wandering inspirations that sing and stray through limpid blue beyond our earthly coasts: and all the land lay deep in the magic of that strange music. And the wild things that Earth has guessed at and the things hidden even from legend were moved to sing age-old songs that their memories had forgotten. And fabulous things of the air were lured downwards out of great heights. And emotions unknown and unthought of troubled the calm of Elfland. The flood of music beat with wonderful waves against the slopes of the grave blue Elfin Mountains, till their precipices uttered strange bronze-like echoes. On Earth no noise was heard of music or echo: not a note came through the narrow border of twilight, not a sound, not a murmur. Elsewhere those notes ascended, and passed like rare strange moths through all the fields of Heaven, and hummed like untraceable memories about the souls of the blessed; and the angels heard that music but were forbidden to envy it. And though it came not to Earth, and though never our fields have heard the music of Elfland, yet there were then as there have been in every age, lest despair should overtake the peoples of Earth, those that make songs for the need of our grief and our laughter: and even they heard never a note from Elfland across the border of twilight that kills their sound, but they felt in their minds the dance of those magical notes, and wrote them down and earthly instruments played them; then and never till then have we heard the music of Elfland.

For a while the Elf King held all things that owed him allegiance, and all their desires and wonders and fears and dreams, floating drowsy on tides of music that was made of no sounds of Earth, but rather of that dim substance in which the planets swim, with many another marvel that only magic knows. And then as all Elfland was drinking the music in, as our Earth drinks in soft rain, he turned again to his daughter with that in his eyes that said "What land is so fair as ours?" And she turned towards him to say "Here is my home forever." Her lips were parted to say it and love was shining in the blue of her elfin eyes; she was stretching her fair hands out towards her father; when they heard the sound of the horn of a tired hunter, wearily blowing by the border of Earth.

Chapter XXVI

The Horn of Alveric

Northward to lonely lands through wearying years Alveric wandered, where windy fragments of his grey gaunt tent added a gloom to chill evenings. And the folk upon lonely farms, as they lit the lights in their houses, and the ricks began to darken against the pale green of the sky, would sometimes hear the rap of the mallets of Niv and Zend coming clear through the hush from the land that no others trod. And their children peering from casements to see if a star was come would see perhaps the queer grey shape of that tent flapping its tatters above the last of the hedgerows, where a moment before was only the grey of the gloaming. On the next morning there would be guesses and wonderings, and the joy and fear of the children, and the tales that their elders told them, and the explorations by stealth to the edge of the fields of men, shy peerings through dim green gaps in the last of the hedgerows (though to look toward the East was forbidden), and rumours and expectations; and all these things were blended together by this wonder that came from the East, and so passed into legend, which lived for many a year beyond that morning; but Alveric and his tent would be gone.

So day by day and season after season that company wandered on, the lonely mateless man, the moonstruck lad and the madman, and that old grey tent with its long twisted pole. And all the stars became known to them, and all the four winds familiar, and rain and mist and hail, but the flow of yellow windows all warm and welcome at night they knew only to say farewell to: with the earliest light in the first chill of dawn Alveric would awake from impatient dreams, and Niv would arise shouting, and away they would go upon their crazed crusade before any sign of awakening appeared on the quiet dim gables. And every morning Niv prophesied that they would surely find Elfland; and the days wore away and the years.

Thyl had long left them; Thyl who prophesied victory to them in burning song, whose inspirations cheered Alveric on coldest nights and led him through rockiest ways, Thyl sang one evening suddenly songs of some young girl's hair, Thyl who should have led their wanderings. And then one day in the gloaming, a blackbird singing, the may in bloom for miles, he turned for the houses of men, and married the maiden and was one no more with any band of wanderers.

The horses were dead; Niv and Zend carried all they had on the pole. Many years had gone. One Autumn morning Alveric left the camp to go to the houses of men. Niv and Zend eyed each other. Why should Alveric seek to ask the way of others? For somehow or other their mad minds knew his purpose more swiftly than sane intuitions. Had he not Niv's prophecies to guide him, and the things that Zend had been told on oath by the full moon?

Alveric came to the houses of men, and of the folk he questioned few would speak at all of things that lay to the East, and if he spoke of the lands through which he had wandered for years they gave as little heed as if he were telling them that he had pitched his tent on the coloured layers of air that glowed and drifted and darkened in the low sky over the sunset. And the few that answered him said one thing only: that only the wizards knew.

When he had learned this Alveric went back from the fields and hedgerows and came again to his old grey tent in the lands of which none thought; and Niv and Zend sat there silent, eying him sideways, for they knew he mistrusted madness and things said by the moon. And next day when they moved their camp in the chill of dawn Niv led the way without shouting.

They had not gone for many more weeks upon their curious journey when Alveric met one morning, at the edge of the fields men tended, one filling his bucket at a well, whose thin high conical hat and mystical air proclaimed him surely a wizard. "Master," said Alveric, "of those arts men dread, I have a question that I would ask of the future."

And the wizard turned from his bucket to look at Alveric with doubtful eyes, for the traveller's tattered figure seemed scarce to promise such fees as are given by those that justly question the future. And, such as those fees are, the wizard named them. And Alveric's wallet held that which banished the doubts of the wizard. So that he pointed to where the tip of his tower peered over a cluster of myrtles, and prayed Alveric to come to his door when the evening star should appear; and in that propitious hour he would make the future clear to him.

And again Niv and Zend knew well that their leader followed after dreams and mysteries that came not from madness nor from the moon. And he left them sitting still and saying nothing, but with minds full of fierce visions.

Through pale air waiting for the evening star Alveric walked over the fields men tended, and came to the dark oak door of the wizard's tower which myrtles brushed against with every breeze. A young apprentice in wizardry opened the door and, by ancient wooden steps that the rats knew better than men, led Alveric to the wizard's upper room.

The wizard had on a silken cloak of black, which he held to be due to the future; without it he would not question the years to be. And when the young apprentice had gone away he moved to a volume he had on a high desk, and turned from the volume to Alveric to ask what he sought of the future. And Alveric asked him how he should come to Elfland. Then the wizard opened the great book's darkened cover and turned the pages therein, and for a long while all the pages he turned were blank, but further on in the book much writing appeared, although of no kind that Alveric had ever seen. And the wizard explained that such books as these told of all things; but that he, being only concerned with the years to be, had no need to read of the past, and had therefore acquired a book that told of the future only; though he might have had more than this from the College of Wizardry, had he cared to study the follies already committed by man.

Then he read for a while in his book, and Alveric heard the rats returning softly to the streets and houses that they had made in the stairs. And then the wizard found what he sought of the future, and told Alveric that it was written in his book how he never should come to Elfland while he carried a magical sword.

When Alveric heard this he paid the wizard's fees and went away doleful. For he knew the perils of Elfland, which no common sabre forged on the anvils of men could ever avail to parry. He did not know that the magic that was in his sword left a flavour or taste on the air like that of lightning, which passed through the border of twilight and spread over Elfland, nor knew that the Elf King learned of his presence thus and drew his frontier away from him, so that Alveric should trouble his realm no more; but he believed what the wizard had read to him out of his book, and so went doleful away. And, leaving the stairs of oak to time and the rats, he passed out of the grove of myrtles and over the fields of men, and came again to that melancholy spot where his grey tent brooded mournfully in the wilderness, dull and silent as Niv and Zend sitting beside it. And after that they turned and wandered southwards, for all journeys now seemed equally hopeless to Alveric, who would not give up his sword to meet magical perils without magical aid; and Niv and Zend obeyed him silently, no longer guiding him with raving prophesies or with things said by the moon, for they knew he had taken counsel with another.

By weary ways with lonely wanderings they came far to the South, and never the border of Elfland appeared with its heavy layers of twilight; yet Alveric would never give up his sword, for well he guessed that Elfland dreaded its magic, and had poor hope of recapturing Lirazel with any blade that was dreadful only to men. And after a while Niv prophesied again, and Zend would come late on nights of the full moon to wake Alveric with his tales. And for all the mystery that was in Zend when he spoke, and for all the exultation of Niv when he prophesied, Alveric knew by now that the tales and the prophecies were empty and vain and that neither of these would ever bring him to Elfland. With this mournful knowledge in a desolate land he still struck camp at dawn, still marched, still sought for the frontier, and so the months went by.

And one day where the edge of Earth was a wild untended heath, running down to the rocky waste in which Alveric had camped, he saw at evening a woman in the hat and cloak of a witch sweeping the heath with a broom. And each stroke as she swept the heath was away from the fields we know, away to the rocky waste, eastwards towards Elfland. Big gusts of black dried earth and puffs of sand were blowing towards Alveric from every powerful stroke. He walked towards her from his sorry encampment and stood near and watched her sweeping; but still she laboured at her vigorous work, striding away behind dust from the fields we know, and sweeping as she strode. And after a while she lifted her face as she swept and looked at Alveric, and he saw that it was the witch Ziroonderel. After all these years he saw that witch again, and she saw beneath the flapping rags of his cloak that sword that she had made for him once on her hill. Its scabbard of leather could not hide from the witch that it was that very sword, for she knew the flavour of magic that rose from it faintly and floated wide through the evening.

"Mother Witch!" said Alveric.

And she curtsied low to him, magical though she was and aged by the passing of years that had been before Alveric's father, and though many in Erl had forgotten their lord by now; yet she had not forgotten.

He asked her what she was doing there, on the heath with her broom in the evening.

"Sweeping the world," she said.

And Alveric wondered what rejected things she was sweeping away from the world, with grey dust mournfully turning over and over as it drifted across our fields, going slowly into the darkness that was gathering beyond our coasts.

"Why are you sweeping the world, Mother Witch?" he said.

"There's things in the world that ought not to be here," said she.

He looked wistfully then at the rolling grey clouds from her broom that were all drifting towards Elfland.

"Mother Witch," he said, "can I go too? I have looked for twelve years for Elfland, and have not found a glimpse of the Elfin Mountains."

And the old witch looked kindly at him, and then she glanced at his sword.

"He's afraid of my magic," she said; and thought or mystery dawned in her eyes as she spoke.

"Who?" said Alveric.

And Ziroonderel lowered her eyes.

"The King," she said.

And then she told him how that enchanted monarch would draw away from whatever had worsted him once, and with him draw all that he had, never supporting the presence of any magic that was the equal of his.

And Alveric could not believe that such a king cared so much for the magic he had in his old black scabbard.

"It is his way," she said.

And then he would not believe that he had waved away Elfland.

"He has the power," said she.

And still Alveric would face this terrible king and all the powers he had; but wizard and witch had warned him that he could not go with his sword, and how go unarmed through the grizzly wood against the palace of wonder? For to go there with any sword from the anvils of men was but to go unarmed.

"Mother Witch," he cried. "May I come no more to Elfland?"

And the longing and grief in his voice touched the witch's heart and moved it to magical pity.

"You shall go," she said.

He stood there half despair in the mournful evening, half dreams of Lirazel. While the witch from under her cloak drew forth a small false weight which once she had taken away from a seller of bread. "Draw this along the edge of your sword," she said, "all the way from hilt to point, and it will disenchant the blade, and the King will never know what sword is there."

"Will it still fight for me?" said Alveric.

"No," said the witch. "But once you are over the frontier take this script and wipe the blade with it on every spot that the false weight has touched." And she fumbled under her cloak again and drew forth a poem on parchment. "It will enchant it again," she said.

And Alveric took the weight and the written thing.

"Let not the two touch," warned the witch.

And Alveric set them apart.

"Once over the frontier," she said, "and he may move Elfland where he will, but you and the sword will be within his borders."

"Mother Witch," said Alveric, "will he be wroth with you if I do this?"

"Wroth!" said Ziroonderel. "Wroth? He will rage with a most exceeding fury, beyond the power of tigers."

"I would not bring that on you, Mother Witch," said Alveric.

"Ha!" said Ziroonderel. "What care I?"

Night was advancing now, and the moor and the air growing black like the witch's cloak. She was laughing now and merging into the darkness. And soon the night was all blackness and laughter; but he could see no witch.

Then Alveric made his way back to his rocky camp by the light of its lonely fire.

And as soon as morning appeared on the desolation, and all the useless rocks began to glow, he took the false weight and softly rubbed it along both sides of his sword until all its magical edge was disenchanted. And he did this in his tent while his followers slept, for he would not let them know that he sought for help that came not from the ravings of Niv, nor from any sayings that Zend had had from the moon.

Yet the troubled sleep of madness is not so deep that Niv did not watch him out of one wild sly eye when he heard the false weight softly rasping the sword.

And when this was secretly done and secretly watched, Alveric called to his two men, and they came and folded up his tattered tent, and took the long pole and hung their sorry belongings upon it; and on went Alveric along the edge of the fields we know, impatient to come at last to the land that so long eluded him. And Niv and Zend came behind with the pole between them, with bundles swinging from it and tatters flying.

They moved inland a little towards the houses of men to purchase the food they needed; and this they bought in the afternoon from a farmer who dwelt in a lonely house, so near to the very edge of the fields we know that it must have been the last house in the visible world. And here they bought bread and oatmeal, and cheese and a cured ham, and other such things, and put them in sacks and slung them over their pole; then they left the farmer and turned away from his fields and from all the fields of men. And as evening fell they saw just over a hedge, lighting up the land with a soft strange glow that they knew to be not of this Earth, that barrier of twilight that is the frontier of Elfland.

"Lirazel!" shouted Alveric, and drew his sword and strode into the twilight. And behind him went Niv and Zend, with all their suspicions flaming now into jealousy of inspirations or magic that were not theirs.

Once he called Lirazel; then, little trusting his voice in that wide weird land, he lifted his hunter's horn that hung by his side on a strap, he lifted it to his lips and sounded a call weary with so much wandering. He was standing within the edge of the boundary; the horn shone in the light of Elfland.

Then Niv and Zend dropped their pole in that unearthly twilight, where it lay like the wreckage of some uncharted sea, and suddenly seized their master.

"A land of dreams!" said Niv. "Have I not dreams enough?"

"There is no moon there!" cried Zend.

Alveric struck Zend on the shoulder with his sword, but the sword was disenchanted and blunt and only harmed him slightly. Then the two seized the sword and dragged Alveric back. And the strength of the madman was beyond what one could believe. They dragged him back again to the fields we know, where they two were strange and were jealous of other strangeness, and led him far from the sight of the pale-blue mountains. He had not entered Elfland.

But his horn had passed the boundary's edge and troubled the air of Elfland, uttering across its dreamy calm one long sad earthly note: it was the horn that Lirazel heard as she spoke with her father.

Chapter XXVII

The Return of Lurulu

Over hamlet and Castle of Erl, and through every nook and crevice of it, Spring passed; a mild benediction that blessed the very air and sought out all living things; not missing even the tiny plants that had their dwelling in most secluded places, under eaves, in the cracks of old barrels, or along the lines of mortar that held ancient rows of stones. And in this season Orion hunted no unicorns; not that he knew in what season the unicorns bred in Elfland, where time is not as here; but because of a feeling he had from all his earthly forefathers against hunting any creature in this season of song and flowers. So he tended his hounds and often watched the hills, expecting on any day the return of Lurulu.

And Spring passed by and the Summer flowers grew, and still there was no sign of the troll returning, for time moves through the dells of Elfland as over no field of man. And long Orion watched through fading evenings till the line of the hills was black, yet never saw the small round heads of trolls bobbing across the downs.

And the long autumnal winds came sighing out of cold lands, and found Orion still watching for Lurulu; and the mist and the turning leaves spoke to his heart of hunting. And the hounds were whining for the open spaces and the line of scent like a mysterious path crossing the wide world, but Orion would hunt nothing less than unicorns, and waited yet for his trolls.

And one of these earthly days, with a menace of frost in the air and a scarlet sunset, Lurulu's talk to the trolls in the wood being finished, and their scamper swifter than hares having brought them soon to the frontier, those in our fields who looked (as they seldom did) towards that mysterious border where Earth ended might have seen the unwonted shapes of the nimble trolls coming all grey through the evening. They came dropping, troll after troll, from the soaring leaps they took high through the boundary of twilight; and, landing thus unceremoniously in our fields, came capering, somersaulting and running, with gusts of impudent laughter, as though this were a proper manner in which to approach by no means the least of the planets.

They rustled by the small houses like the wind passing through straw, and none that heard the light rushing sound of their passing knew how outlandish they were, except the dogs, whose work it is to watch, and who know of all things that pass, their degree of remoteness to man. At gipsies, tramps, and all that go without houses, dogs bark whenever they pass; at the wild things of the woods they bark with greater abhorrence, knowing well the rebellious contempt in which they hold man; at the fox, for his touch of mystery and his far wanderings, they bark more furiously: but to-night the barking of dogs was beyond all abhorrence and fury; many a farmer this night believed that his dog was choking.

And passing over these fields, staying not to laugh at the clumsy scared running of sheep, for they kept their laughter for man, they came soon to the downs above Erl; and there below them was night and the smoke of men, all grey together. And not knowing from what slight causes the smoke arose, here from a woman boiling a kettle of water, or there because one dried the frock of a child, or that a few old men might warm their hands in the evening, the trolls forbore to laugh as they had planned to do as soon as they should meet with the things of man. Perhaps even they, whose gravest thoughts were just under the surface of laughter, even they were a little awed by the strangeness and nearness of man sleeping there in his hamlet with all his smoke about him. Though awe in these light minds rested no longer than does the squirrel on the thin extremest twigs.

In a while they lifted their eyes up from the valley, and there was the western sky still shining above the last of the gloaming, a little strip of colour and dying light, so lovely that they believed that another elfland lay the other side of the valley, two dim diaphonous magical elfin lands hemming in this valley and few fields of men close upon either side. And, sitting there on the hillside peering westward, the next thing they saw was a star: it was Venus low in the West brimming with blueness. And they all bowed their heads many times to this pale-blue beautiful stranger; for though politeness was rare with them they saw that the Evening Star was nothing of Earth and no affair of man's, and believed it came out of that elfland they did not know on the western side of the world. And more and more stars appeared, till the trolls were frightened, for they knew nothing of these glittering wanderers that could steal out of the darkness and shine: at first they said "There are more trolls than stars," and were comforted, for they trusted greatly in numbers. Then there were soon more stars than trolls; and the trolls were ill at ease as they sat in the dark underneath all that multitude. But presently they forgot the fancy that troubled them, for no thought remained with them long. They turned their light attention instead to the yellow lights that glowed here and there on the hither side of the greyness, where a few of the houses of men stood warm and snug near the trolls. A beetle went by, and they hushed their chatter to hear what he would say; but he droned by, going home, and they did not know his language. A dog far off was ceaselessly crying out, and filling all the still night with a note of warning. And the trolls were angry at the sound of his voice, for they felt that he interfered between them and man. Then a soft whiteness came out of the night and lit on the branch of a tree, and bowed its head to the left and looked at the trolls, and then bowed over to the right and looked at them again from there, and then back to the left again for it was not yet sure about them. "An owl," said Lurulu; and many besides Lurulu had seen his kind before, for he flies much along the edge of Elfland. Soon he was gone and they heard him hunting across the hills and the hollows; and then no sound was left but the voices of men, or the shrill shouts of children, and the bay of the dog that warned men against the trolls. "A sensible fellow," they said of the owl, for they liked the sound of his voice; but the voices of men and their dog sounded confused and tiresome.

They saw sometimes the lights of late wayfarers crossing the downs towards Erl, or heard men that cheered themselves in the lonely night by singing, instead of by lantern's light. And all the while the Evening Star grew bigger, and great trees grew blacker and blacker.

Then from underneath the smoke and the mist of the stream there boomed all of a sudden the brazen bell of the Freer out of deep night in the valley. Night and the slopes of Erl and the dark downs echoed with it; and the echoes rode up to the trolls and seemed to challenge them, with all accursed things and wandering spirits and bodies unblessed of the Freer.

And the solemn sound of those echoes going alone through the night from every heavy swing of the holy bell cheered that band of trolls among all the strangeness of Earth, for whatever is solemn always moves trolls to levity. They turned merrier now and tittered among themselves.

And while they still watched all that host of stars, wondering if they were friendly, the sky grew steely blue and the eastern stars dwindled, and the mist and the smoke of men turned white, and a radiance touched the further edge of the valley; and the moon came up over the downs behind the trolls. Then voices sang from the holy place of the Freer, chaunting moon matins; which it was their wont to sing on nights of the full moon while the moon was yet low. And this rite they named moon's-morning. The bell had ceased, chance voices spoke no more, they had hushed their dog in the valley and silenced his warning, and lonely and grave and solemn that people's song floated up from before the candles in their small square sacred place, built of grey stone by men that were dead for ages and ages; all solemn the song welled up in the time of the moon's rising, grave as the night, mysterious as the full moon, and fraught with a meaning that was far beyond the highest thoughts of the trolls. Then the trolls leaped up with one accord from the frosted grass of the downs and all poured down the valley to laugh at the ways of men, to mock at their sacred things and to dare their singing with levity.

Many a rabbit rose up and fled from their onrush, and thrills of laughter arose from the trolls at their fear. A meteor flashed westwards, racing after the sun; either as a portent to warn the hamlet of Erl that folk from beyond Earth's borders approached them now, or else in fulfilment of some natural law. To the trolls it seemed that one of the proud stars fell, and they rejoiced with elvish levity.

Thus they came giggling through the night, and ran down the street of the village, unseen as any wild creature that roams late through the darkness; and Lurulu led them to the pigeon-loft, and they all poured clambering in. Some rumour arose in the village that a fox had jumped into the pigeon-loft, but it ceased almost as soon as the pigeons returned to their homes, and the folk of Erl had no more hint till the morning that something had entered their village from beyond the borders of Earth.

In a brown mass thicker than young pigs are along the edge of a trough the trolls encumbered the floor of the pigeons' home. And time went over them as over all earthly things. And well they knew, though tiny was their intelligence, that by crossing the border of twilight they incurred the wasting of time; for nothing dwells by the brink of any danger and lives ignorant of its menace: as conies in rocky altitudes know the peril of the sheer cliff, so they that dwell near Earth's border knew well the danger of time. And yet they came. The wonder and lure of Earth had been overstrong for them. Does not many a young man squander youth as they squandered immortality?

And Lurulu showed them how to hold off time for a while, which otherwise would make them older and older each moment and whirl them on with Earth's restlessness all night long. Then he curled up his knees and shut his eyes and lay still. This, he told them, was sleep; and, cautioning them to continue to breathe, though being still in other respects, he then slept in earnest: and after some vain attempts the brown trolls did the same.

When sunrise came, awaking all earthly things, long rays came through the thirty little windows and awoke both birds and trolls. And the mass of trolls went to the windows to look at Earth, and the pigeons fluttered to rafters and jerked sidelong looks at the trolls. And there that heap of trolls would have stayed, crowded high on each other's shoulders, blocking the windows while they studied the variety and restlessness of Earth, finding them equal to the strangest fables that wayfarers had brought to them out of our fields; and, though Lurulu often reminded them, they had forgotten the haughty white unicorns that they were to hunt with dogs.

But Lurulu after a while led them down from the loft and brought them to the kennels. And they climbed up the high palings and peered over the top at the hounds.

When the hounds saw those strange heads peering over the palings they made a great uproar. And presently folk came to see what troubled the hounds. And when they saw that mass of trolls all round the top of the palings they said to each other, and so said all that heard of it: "There is magic in Erl now."

Chapter XXVIII

A Chapter on Unicorn-Hunting

None in Erl was so busy but that he came that morning to see the magic that was newly come out of Elfland, and to compare the trolls with all that the neighbours said of them. And the folk of Erl gazed much at the trolls and the trolls at the folk of Erl, and there was great merriment; for, as often happens with minds of unequal weight, each laughed at the other. And the villagers found the impudent ways of the bare brown nimble trolls no funnier, no more meet for derision, than the trolls found the grave high hats, the curious clothes, and the solemn air of the villagers.

And Orion soon came too, and the folk of the village doffed their long thin hats; and, though the trolls would have laughed at him also, Lurulu had found his whip, and by means of it made the mob of his impudent brethren give that salutation that is given in Elfland to those of its royal line.

When noonday came, which was the hour of dinner, and the folk turned from the kennels, they went back to their houses all praising the magic that was come at last to Erl.

During the days that followed Orion's hounds learned that it was vain to chase a troll and unwise to snarl at one; for, apart from their elvish speed, the trolls were able to leap into the air far over the heads of the hounds, and when each had been given a whip they could repay snarling with an aim that none on Earth was able to equal, except those whose sires had carried a whip with hounds for generations.

And one morning Orion came to the pigeon-loft and called to Lurulu early, and he brought out the trolls and they went to the kennels and Orion opened the doors, and he led them all away eastwards over the downs. The hounds moved all together and the trolls with their whips ran beside them, like a flock of sheep surrounded by numbers of collies. They were away to the border of Elfland to wait for the unicorns where they come through the twilight to eat the earthly grasses at evening. And as our evening began to mellow the fields we know, they were come to the opal border that shut those fields from Elfland. And there they lurked as Earth's darkness grew, and waited for the great unicorns. Each hound had its troll beside it with the troll's right

still haunting Unicorns

hand along its shoulder or neck, soothing it, calming it, and holding it still, while the left hand held the whip: the strange group lingered there motionless, and darkened there with the evening. And when Earth was as dim and quiet as the unicorns desired the great creatures came softly through, and were far into Earth before any troll would allow his hound to move. Thus when Orion gave the signal they easily cut one off from its elfin home and hunted it snorting over those fields that are the portion of men. And night came down on the proud beast's magical gallop, and the hounds intoxicate with that marvellous scent, and the leaping soaring trolls.

And, when jackdaws on the highest towers of Erl saw the rim of the sun all red above frosted fields, Orion came back from the downs with his hounds and his trolls, carrying as fine a head as a unicorn-hunter could wish. The hounds weary but glad were soon curled up in their kennels, and Orion in his bed; while the trolls in their pigeon-loft began to feel, as none but Lurulu had felt ever before, the weight and the weariness of the passing of time.

All day Orion slept and all his hounds, none of them caring how it slept or why; while the trolls slept anxiously, falling asleep as fast as ever they could, in the hope of escaping some of the fury of time, which they feared had begun to attack them. And that evening while still they slept, hounds, trolls and Orion, there met again in the forge of Narl the parliament of Erl.

From the forge to the inner room came the twelve old men, rubbing their hands and smiling, ruddy with health and the keen North wind and the cheerfulness of their forebodings; for they were well content at last that their lord was surely magic, and foresaw great doings in Erl.

"Folklings," said Narl to them all, naming them thus after an ancient wont, "is it not well with us and our valley at last? See how it is as we planned so long ago. For our lord is a magic lord as we all desired, and magical things have sought him from over there, and they all obey his hests."

"It is so," said all but Gazic, a vendor of beeves.

Little and old and out-of-the-way was Erl, secluded in its deep valley, unnoticed in history; and the twelve men loved the place and would have it famous. And now they rejoiced as they heard the words of Narl, "What other village," he said, "has traffic with over there?"

And Gazic, though he rejoiced with the rest, rose up in a pause of their gladness. "Many strange things," he said, "have entered our village, coming from over there. And it may be that human folk are best, and the ways of the fields we know."

Oth scorned him, and Threl. "Magic is best," said all.

And Gazic was silent again, and raised his voice no more against the many; and the mead went round, and all spoke of the fame of Erl;

and Gazic forgot his mood and the fear that was in it.

Far into the night they rejoiced, quaffing the mead, and by its homely aid gazing into the years of the future, so far as that may be done by the eyes of men. Yet all their rejoicing was hushed and their voices low, lest the ears of the Freer should hear them; for their gladness came to them from lands that lay beyond thought of salvation, and they had set their trust in magic, against which, as well they knew, boomed every note that rang from the bell of the Freer whenever it tolled at evening. And they parted late, praising magic in no loud tones, and went secretly back to their houses, for they feared the curse that the Freer had called down upon unicorns, and knew not if their own names might become involved in one of the curses called upon magical things.

All the next day Orion rested his hounds, and the trolls and the people of Erl gazed at each other. But on the day that followed Orion took his sword and gathered his band of trolls and his pack of hounds, and all were away once more far over the downs, to come again to the border of nebulous opal and to lurk for the unicorns coming through in the evening.

They came to a part of the border far from the spot which they had disturbed only three evenings before; and Orion was guided by the chattering trolls, for well they knew the haunts of the lonely unicorns. And Earth's evening came huge and hushed, till all was dim as the twilight; and never a footfall did they hear of the unicorns, never a glimpse of their whiteness. And yet the trolls had guided Orion well, for just as he would have despaired of a hunt that night, just when the evening seemed wholly and utterly empty, a unicorn stood on the earthward edge of the twilight where nothing had stood only a moment before: soon he moved slowly across the terrestrial grasses a few yards forward into the fields of men.

Another followed, moving a few yards also; and then they stood for fifteen of our earthly minutes moving nothing at all except their ears. And all that while the trolls hushed every hound, motionless under a hedge of the fields we know. Darkness had all but hidden them when at last the unicorns moved. And, as soon as the largest was far enough from the frontier, the trolls let loose every hound, and ran with them after the unicorn with shrill yells of derision, all sure of his haughty head.

But the quick small minds of the trolls, though they had learned much of Earth, had not yet understood the irregularity of the moon. Darkness was new to them, and they soon lost hounds. Orion in his eagerness to hunt had made no choice of a suitable night: there was no moon at all, and would be none till near morning. Soon he also fell behind.

Orion easily collected the trolls, the night was full of their frivolous noises, and the trolls came to his horn, but not a hound would leave that pungent magical scent for any horn of man. They straggled back next day, tired, having lost their unicorn.

And while each troll cleaned and fed his hound on the evening after the hunt, and laid a little bunch of straw for it on which to lie down, and smoothed its hair and looked for thorns in its feet, and unravelled burrs from its ears, Lurulu sat alone fastening his small sharp intelligence, like the little white light of a burning glass, for hours upon one question. The question that Lurulu pondered far into the night was how to hunt unicorns with dogs in the darkness. And by midnight a plan was clear in his elvish mind.

Chapter XXIX

The Luring of the People of the Marshes

As the evening that followed was beginning to fade a traveller might have been seen approaching the marshes, which some way south-eastwards of Erl lay along the edge of the farmsteads and stretched their terrible waste as far as the sky-line, and even over the border and into the region of Elfland. They glimmered now as the light was leaving the land.

So black were the solemn clothes and the high grave hat of the traveller that he could have been seen from far against the dim green of the fields, going down to the edge of the marsh through the grey evening. But none were there to see at such an hour beside that desolate place, for the threat of darkness was already felt in the fields, and all the cows were home and the farmers warm in their houses; so the traveller walked alone. And soon he was come by unsure paths to the reeds and the thin rushes, to which a wind was telling tales that have no meaning to man, long histories of bleakness and ancient legends of rain; while on the high darkening land far off behind him he saw lights begin to blink where the houses were. He walked with the gravity and the solemn air of one who has important business with men; yet his back was turned to their houses and he went where no man wandered, travelling towards no hamlet or lonely cottage of man, for the marsh ran right into Elfland. Between him and the nebulous border that divides Earth from Elfland there was no man whatever, and yet the traveller walked on as one that has a grave errand. With every venerable step that he took bright mosses shook and the marsh seemed about to engulf him, while his worthy staff sank deep into slime, giving him no support; and yet the traveller seemed only to care for the solemnity of his pacing. Thus he went on over the deadly marsh with a deportment suitable to the slow procession when the elders open the market on special days, and the gravest blesses the bargaining, and all the farmers come to the booths and barter.

And up and down, up and down, song-birds went wavering home, skirting the marsh's edge on their way to their native hedges; pigeons passed landward to roost in high dark trees; the last of a multitude of rooks was gone; and all the air was empty.

And now the great marsh thrilled to the news of the coming of a stranger; for, no sooner had the traveller gravely set a foot on one of those brilliant mosses that bloom in the pools, than a thrill shot under their roots and below the stems of the bulrushes, and ran like a light beneath the surface of the water, or like the sound of a song, and passed far over the marshes, and came quivering to the border of magical twilight that divides Elfland from Earth; and stayed not there, but troubled the very border and passed beyond it and was felt in Elfland: for where the great marshes run down to the border of Earth the frontier is thinner and more uncertain than elsewhere.

And as soon as they felt that thrill in the deep of the marshes the will-o'-the-wisps soared up from their fathomless homes, and waved their lights to beckon the traveller on, over the quaking mosses at the hour when the duck were flighting. And under that whirr and rush and rejoicing of wings that the ducks make in that hour the traveller followed after the waving lights, further and further into the marshes. Yet sometimes he turned from them, so that for a while they followed him, instead of leading as they were accustomed to do, till they could get round in front of him and lead him once more. A watcher, if there had been one in such bad light and in such a perilous place, had noticed after a while in the venerable traveller's movements a queer resemblance to those of the hen green plover when she lures the stranger after her in Spring, away from the mossy bank where her eggs lie bare. Or perhaps such a resemblance is merely fanciful, and a watcher might have noticed no such thing. At any rate on that night in that desolate place there was no watcher whatever.

And the traveller followed his curious course, sometimes towards the dangerous mosses, sometimes towards the safe green land, always with grave demeanour and reverent gait; and the will-o'-the-wisps in multitudes gathered about him. And still that deep thrill that warned the marsh of a stranger throbbed on through the ooze below the roots of the rushes; and did not cease, as it should as soon as the stranger was dead, but haunted the marsh like some echo of music that magic has made everlasting, and troubled the will-o'-the-wisps even over the border in Elfland.

Now it is far from my intention to write anything detrimental to will-o'-the-wisps, or anything that may be construed as being a slight upon them: no such construction should be put upon my writings. But it is well known that the people of the marshes lure travellers to their doom, and have delighted to follow that avocation for centuries, and I may be permitted to mention this in no spirit of disapproval.

The will-o'-the-wisps then that were about this traveller redoubled their efforts with fury; and when still he eluded their last enticements only on the very edge of the deadliest pools, and still lived and still travelled, and the whole marsh knew of it, then the greater will-o'-the-wisps that dwell in Elfland rose up from their magical mire and rushed over the border. And the whole marsh was troubled.

Almost like little moons grown nimbly impudent the people of the marshes glowed before that solemn traveller, leading his reverend steps to the edge of death only to retrace their steps again to beckon him back once more. And then in spite of the great height of his hat and the dark length of his coat that frivolous people began to perceive that mosses were bearing his weight which never before had supported any traveller. At this their fury increased and they all leaped nearer to him; and nearer and nearer they flocked wherever he went; and in their fury their enticements were losing their craftiness.

And now a watcher in the marshes, if such there had been, had seen something more than a traveller surrounded by will-o'-the-wisps; for he might have noticed that the traveller was almost leading them, instead of the will-o'-the-wisps leading the traveller. And in their impatience to have him dead the people of the marshes had never thought that they were all coming nearer and nearer to the dry land.

And when all was dark but the water they suddenly found themselves in a field of grass with their feet rasping against the rough pasture, while the traveller was seated with his knees gathered up to his chin and was eyeing them from under the brim of his high black hat. Never before had any of them been lured to dry land by traveller, and there were amongst them that night those eldest and greatest among them who had come with their moon-like lights right over the border from Elfland. They looked at each other in uneasy astonishment as they dropped limply onto the grass, for the roughness and heaviness of the solid land oppressed them after the marshes. And then they began to perceive that that venerable traveller whose bright eyes watched them so keenly out of that black mass of clothes was little larger than they were themselves, in spite of his reverend airs. Indeed, though stouter and rounder he was not quite so tall. Who was this, they began to mutter, who had lured will-o'-the-wisps? And some of those elders from Elfland went up to him that they might ask him with what audacity he had dared to lure such as them. And then the traveller spoke. Without rising or turning his head he spoke where he sat.

"People of the marshes," he said, "do you love unicorns?"

And at the word unicorns scorn and laughter filled every tiny heart in all that frivolous multitude, excluding all other emotions, so that they forgot their petulance at having been lured; although to lure will-o'-the-wisps is held by them to be the gravest of insults, and never would they have forgiven it if they had had longer memories. At the word unicorns they all giggled in silence. And this they did by flickering up and down like the light of a little mirror flashed by an impudent hand. Unicorns! Little love had they for the haughty creatures. Let them learn to speak to the people of the marshes when they came to drink at their pools. Let them learn to give their due to the great lights of Elfland, and the lesser lights that illumined the marshes of Earth!

"No," said an elder of the will-o'-the-wisps, "none loves the proud unicorns."

"Come then," said the traveller, "and we will hunt them. And you shall light us in the night with your lights, when we hunt them with dogs over the fields of men."

"Venerable traveller," said that elder will-o'-the-wisp: but at those words the traveller flung up his hat and leaped from his long black coat, and stood before the will-o'-the-wisps stark naked. And the people of the marshes saw that it was a troll that had tricked them.

Their anger at this was slight; for the people of the marshes have tricked the trolls, and the trolls have tricked the people of the marshes, each of them so many times for ages and ages, that only the wisest among them can say which has tricked the other most and is how many tricks ahead. They consoled themselves now by thinking of times when trolls had been made to look ludicrous, and consented to come with their lights to help to hunt unicorns, for their wills were weak when they stood on the dry land and they easily acquiesced in any suggestion or followed anyone's whim.

It was Lurulu who had thus tricked the will-o'-the-wisps, knowing well how they love to lure travellers; and, having obtained the highest hat and gravest coat he could steal, he had set out with a bait that he knew would bring them from great distances. Now that he had gathered them all on the solid land and had their promise of light and help against unicorns, which such creatures will give easily on account of the unicorns' pride, he began to lead them away to the village of Erl, slowly at first while their feet grew accustomed to the hard land; and over the fields he brought them limping to Erl.

And now there was nothing in all the marshes that at all resembled man, and the geese came down on a huge tumult of wings. The little swift teal shot home; and all the dark air twanged with the flight of the duck.

Chapter XXX

The Coming of Too Much Magic

In Erl that had sighed for magic there was indeed magic now. The pigeon-loft and old lumber-lofts over stables were all full of trolls, the ways were full of their antics, and lights bobbed up and down the street at night long after traffic was home. For the will-o'-the-wisps would go dancing along the gutters, and had made their homes round the soft edges of duck-ponds and in green-black patches of moss that grew upon oldest thatch. And nothing seemed the same in the old village.

And amongst all these magical folk the magical half of Orion's blood, that had slept while he went amongst earthly men, hearing mundane talk each day, stirred out of its sleep and awakened long-sleeping thoughts in his brain. And the elfin horns that he often heard blowing at evening blew with a meaning now, and blew stronger as though they were nearer.

The folk of the village watching their lord by day saw his eyes turned away towards Elfland, saw him neglecting the wholesome earthly cares, and at night there came the queer lights and the gibbering of the trolls. A fear settled on Erl.

At this time the parliament took counsel again, twelve grey-beard quaking men that had come to the house of Narl when their work was ended at evening; and all the evening was weird with the new magic of Elfland. Every man of them as he ran from his own warm house on his way to the forge of Narl had seen lights leaping, or heard voices gibbering, which were of no Christom land. And some had seen shapes prowling which were of no earthly growing, and they feared that all manner of things had slipped through the border of Elfland to come and visit the trolls.

They spoke low in their parliament: all told the same tale, a tale of children terrified, a tale of women demanding the old ways again; and as they spoke they eyed window and crevice, none knowing what might come.

And Oth said: "Let us folk go to the Lord Orion as we went to his grandfather in his long red room. Let us say how we sought for magic, and lo we have magic enough; and let him follow no more after witchery nor the things that are hidden from man."

He listened acutely, standing there amongst his hushed comrade neighbours. Was it goblin voices that mocked him, or was it only echo? Who could say? And almost at once the night all round was hushed again.

And Threl said: "Nay. It is too late for that." Threl had seen their lord one evening standing alone on the downs, all motionless and listening to something sounding from Elfland, with his eyes to the East as he listened: and nothing was sounding, not a noise was astir; yet Orion stood there called by things beyond mortal hearing. "It is too late now," said Threl.

And that was the fear of all.

Then Guhic rose slowly up and stood by that table. And trolls were gibbering like bats away in their loft, and the pale marsh-lights were flickering, and shapes prowled in the dark: the pit-pat of their feet came now and then to the ears of the twelve that were there in that inner room. And Guhic said: "We wished for a little magic." And a gust of gibbering came clear from the trolls. And then they disputed awhile as to how much magic they had wished in the olden time, when the grandfather of Orion was lord in Erl. But when they came to a plan this was the plan of Guhic.

"If we may not turn our lord Orion," he said, "and his eyes be turned to Elfland, let all our parliament go up the hill to the witch Ziroonderel, and put our case to her, and ask for a spell which shall be put against too much magic."

And at the name of Ziroonderel the twelve took heart again; for they knew that her magic was greater than the magic of flickering lights, and knew there was not a troll or thing of the night but went in fear of her broom. They took heart again and quaffed Narl's heavy mead, and re-filled their mugs and praised Guhic.

And late in the night they all rose up together to go back to their homes, and all kept close together as they went, and sang grave old songs to affright the things that they feared; though little the light trolls care, or the will-o'-the-wisps, for the things that are grave to man. And when only one was left he ran to his house, and the will-o'-the-wisps chased him.

When the next day came they ended their work early, for the parliament of Erl cared not to be left on the witch's hill when night came, or even the gloaming. They met outside Narl's forge in the early afternoon, eleven of the parliament, and they called out Narl. And all were wearing the clothes they were wont to wear when they went with the rest to the holy place of the Freer, though there was scarcely a soul he had ever cursed that was not blessed by her. And away they went with their old stout staves up the hill.

And as soon as they could they came to the witch's house. And there they found her sitting outside her door gazing over the valley away, and looking neither older nor younger, nor concerned one way or the other with the coming and going of years.

"We be the parliament of Erl," they said, standing before her all in their graver clothes.

"Aye," she said. "You desired magic. Has it come to you yet?"

"Truly," they said, "and to spare."

"There is more to come," she said.

"Mother Witch," said Narl, "we are met here to pray you that you will give us a goodly spell which shall be a charm against magic, so that there be no more of it in the valley, for overmuch has come."

"Overmuch?" she said. "Overmuch magic! As though magic were not the spice and essence of life, its ornament and its splendour. By my broom," said she, "I give you no spell against magic."

And they thought of the wandering lights and the scarce-seen gibbering things, and all the strangeness and evil that was come to their valley of Erl, and they besought her again, speaking suavely to her.

"Oh, Mother Witch," said Guhic, "there is overmuch magic indeed, and the folk that should tarry in Elfland are all over the border."

"It is even so," said Narl. "The border is broken and there will be no end to it. Will-o'-the-wisps should stay in the marshes, and trolls and goblins in Elfland, and we folk should keep to our own folk. This is the thought of us all. For magic, if we desired it somewhat, years ago when we were young, pertains to matters that are not for man."

She eyed him silently with a cat-like glow increasing in her eyes. And when she neither spoke nor moved, Narl besought her again.

"O Mother Witch," he said, "will you give us no spell to guard our homes against magic?"

"No spell indeed!" she hissed. "No spell indeed! By broom and stars and night-riding! Would you rob Earth of her heirloom that has come from the olden time? Would you take her treasure and leave her bare to the scorn of her comrade planets? Poor indeed were we without magic, whereof we are well stored to the envy of darkness and Space." She leaned forward from where she sat and stamped her stick, looking up in Narl's face with her fierce unwavering eyes. "I would sooner," she said, "give you a spell against water, that all the world should thirst, than give you a spell against the song of streams that evening hears faintly over the ridge of a hill, too dim for wakeful ears, a song threading through dreams, whereby we learn of old wars and lost loves of the Spirits of rivers. I would sooner give you a spell against bread, that all the world should starve, than give you a spell against the magic of wheat that haunts the golden hollows in moonlight in July, through which in the warm short nights wander how many of whom man knows nothing. I would make you spells against comfort and clothing, food, shelter and warmth, aye and will do it, sooner than tear from these poor fields of Earth that magic that is to them an ample cloak against the chill of Space, and a gay raiment against the sneers of nothingness.

"Go hence. To your village go. And you that sought for magic in your youth but desire it not in your age, know that there is a blindness of spirit which comes from age, more black than the blindness of eye, making a darkness about you across which nothing may be seen, or felt, or known, or in any way apprehended. And no voice out of that darkness shall conjure me to grant a spell against magic. Hence!"

And as she said "Hence" she put her weight on her stick and was evidently preparing to rise from her seat. And at this great terror came upon all the parliament. And they noticed at the same moment that evening was drawing in and all the valley darkening. On this high field where the witch's cabbages grew some light yet lingered, and listening to her fierce words they had not thought of the hour. But now it was manifestly growing late, and a wind roamed past them that seemed to come over the ridges a little way off, from night; and chilled them as it passed; and all the air seemed given over to that very thing against which they sought for a spell.

And here they were at this hour with the witch before them, and she was evidently about to rise. Her eyes were fixed on them. Already she was partly up from her chair. There could be no doubt that before three moments were passed she would be hobbling amongst them with her glittering eyes peering in each one's face. They turned and ran down the hill.

Chapter XXXI

The Cursing of Elfin Things

As the parliament of Erl ran down the hill they ran into the dusk of evening. Greyly it lay in the valley above the mist from the stream. But with more than the mystery of dusk the air was heavy. Lights blinking early from houses showed that all the folk were home, and the street was deserted by everything that was human; save when with hushed air and almost furtive step they saw their lord Orion like a tall shadow go by, with will-o'-the-wisps behind him, towards the house of the trolls, thinking no earthly thoughts. And the strangeness that had been growing day by day made all the village eerie. So that with short and troubled breath the twelve old men hurried on.

And so they came to the holy place of the Freer, which lay on the side of the village that was towards the witch's hill. And it was the hour at which he was wont to celebrate after-bird-song, as they named the singing that they sang in the holy place when all the birds were home. But the Freer was not within his holy place; he stood in the cold night air on the upper step without it, his face turned towards Elfland. He had on his sacred robe with its border of purple, and the emblem of gold round his neck; but the door of his holy place was shut and his back was towards it. They wondered to see him stand thus.

And as they wondered the Freer began to intone, clear in the evening with his eyes away to the East, where already a few of the earliest stars were showing. With his head held high he spoke as though his voice might pass over the frontier of twilight and be heard by the people of Elfland.

"Curst be all wandering things," he said, "whose place is not upon Earth. Curst be all lights that dwell in fens and in marish places. Their homes are in deeps of the marshes. Let them by no means stir from there until the Last Day. Let them abide in their place and there await damnation.

"Cursed be gnomes, trolls, elves and goblins on land, and all sprites of the water. And fauns be accursed and such as follow Pan. And all that dwell on the heath, being other than beasts or men. Cursed be fairies and all tales told of them, and whatever enchants the meadows before the sun is up, and all fables of doubtful authority, and the legends that men hand down from unhallowed times.

"Cursed be brooms that leave their place by the hearth. Cursed be witches and all manner of witcheries.

"Cursed be toadstool rings and whatever dances within them. And all strange lights, strange songs, strange shadows, or rumours that hint of them, and all doubtful things of the dusk, and the things that ill-instructed children fear, and old wives' tales and things done o' midsummer nights; all these be accursed with all that leaneth toward Elfland and all that cometh thence."

Never a lane of that village, never a barn, but a will-o'-the-wisp was dancing nimbly above it; the night was gilded with them. But as the good Freer spoke they backed away from his curses, floating further off as though a light wind blew them, and danced again after drifting a little way. This they did both before and behind him and upon either hand, as he stood there upon the steps of his holy place. So that there was a circle of darkness all round him, and beyond that circle shone the lights of the marshes and Elfland.

And within the dark circle in which the Freer stood making his curses were no unhallowed things, nor were there strangenesses such as come of night, nor whispers from unknown voices, nor sounds of any music blowing here from no haunts of men; but all was orderly and seemly there and no mysteries troubled the quiet except such as have been justly allowed to man.

And beyond that circle whence so much was beaten back by the bright vehemence of the good man's curses, the will-o'-the-wisps rioted, and many a strangeness that poured in that night from Elfland, and goblins held high holiday. For word was gone forth in Elfland that pleasant folk had now their dwelling in Erl; and many a thing of fable, many a monster of myth, had crept through that border of twilight and had come into Erl to see. And the light and false but friendly will-o'-the-wisps danced in the haunted air and made them welcome.

And not only the trolls and the will-o'-the-wisps had lured these folk from their fabled land through the seldom-traversed border, but the longings and thoughts of Orion, which by half his lineage were akin to the things of myth and of one race with the monsters of Elfland, were calling to them now. Ever since that day by the frontier when he had hovered between Earth and Elfland he had yearned more and more for his mother; and now, whether he willed it or no, his elfin thoughts were calling their kin that dwelt in the elvish fells; and at that hour when the sound of the horns blew through the frontier of twilight they had come tumbling after it. For elfin thoughts are as much akin to the creatures that dwell in Elfland as goblins are to trolls.

Within the calm and the dark of the good man's curses the twelve old men stood silent listening to every word. And the words seemed good to them and soothing and right, for they were over-weary of magic.

But beyond the circle of darkness, amidst the glare of the will-o'-the-wisps with which all the night flickered, amidst goblin laughter and the unbridled mirth of the trolls, where old legends seemed alive and the fearfullest fables true; amongst all manner of mysteries, queer sounds, queer shapes, and queer shadows; Orion passed with his hounds, eastwards towards Elfland.

Chapter XXXII

Lirazel Yearns for Earth

In the hall that was built of moonlight, dreams, music and mirage Lirazel knelt on the sparkling floor before her father's throne. And the light of the magical throne shone blue in her eyes, and her eyes flashed back a light that deepened its magic. And kneeling there she besought a rune of her father.

Old days would not let her be, sweet memories thronged about her: the lawns of Elfland had her love, lawns upon which she had played by the old miraculous flowers before any histories were written here; she loved the sweet soft creatures of myth that moved like magical shadows out of the guardian wood and over enchanted grasses; she loved every fable and song and spell that had made her elfin home; and yet the bells of Earth, that could not pass the frontier of silence and twilight, beat note by note in her brain, and her heart felt the growth of the little earthly flowers as they bloomed or faded or slept in seasons that came not to Elfland. And in those seasons, wasting away as every one went by, she knew that Alveric wandered, knew that Orion lived and grew and changed, and that both, if Earth's legend were true, would soon be lost to her forever and ever, when the gates of Heaven would shut on both with a golden thud. For between Elfland and Heaven is no path, no flight, no way; and neither sends ambassador to the other. She yearned to the bells of Earth and the English cowslips, but would not forsake again her mighty father nor the world that his mind had made. And

Alveric came not, nor her boy Orion; only the sound of Alveric's horn came once, and often strange longings seemed to float in air, beating vainly back and forth between Orion and her. And the gleaming pillars that held the dome of the roof, or above which it floated, quivered a little with her grief; and shadows of her sorrow flickered and faded in the crystal deep of the walls, for a moment dimming many a colour that is unknown in our fields, but making them no less lovely. What could she do who would not cast away magic and leave the home that an ageless day had endeared to her while centuries were withering like leaves upon earthly shores, whose heart was yet held by those little tendrils of Earth, which are strong enough, strong enough?

And some, translating her bitter need into pitiless earthly words, may say that she wished to be in two places at once. And that was true, and the impossible wish lies on the verge of laughter, and for her was only and wholly a matter for tears. Impossible? Was it impossible? We have to do with magic.

She besought a rune of her father, kneeling upon the magic floor in the midmost centre of Elfland; and around her arose the pillars, of which only song may say, whose misty bulk was disturbed and troubled by Lirazel's sorrow. She besought a rune that, wherever they roamed through whatever fields of Earth, should restore to her Alveric and Orion, bringing them over the border and into the elfin lands to live in that timeless age that is one long day in Elfland. And with them she prayed might come, (for the mighty runes of her father had such power even as this) some garden of Earth, or bank where violets lay, or hollow where cowslips waved, to shine in Elfland for ever.

Like no music heard in any cities of men or dreamed upon earthly hills, with his elfin voice her father answered her. And the ringing words were such as had power to change the shape of the hills of dreams, or to enchant new flowers to blow in fields of faery. "I have no rune," he said, "that has power to pass the frontier, or to lure anything from the mundane fields, be it violets, cowslips or men, to come through our bulwark of twilight that I have set to guard us against material things. No rune but one, and that the last of the potencies of our realm."

And kneeling yet upon the glittering floor, of whose profound translucence song alone shall speak, she prayed him for that one rune, last potency though it be of the awful wonders of Elfland.

And he would not squander that rune that lay locked in his treasury, most magical of his powers and last of the three, but held it against the peril of a distant and unknown day, whose light shone just beyond a curve of the ages, too far for the eerie vision even of his foreknowledge.

She knew that he had moved Elfland far afield and swung it back as tides are swung by the moon, till it lapped at the very edge of the fields of men once more, with its glimmering border touching the tips of the earthly hedges. And she knew that no more than the moon had he used a rare wonder, merely wafting his regions away by a magical gesture. Might he not, she thought, bring Elfland and Earth yet nearer, using no rarer magic than is used by the moon at the neap? And so she supplicated him once again, recalling wonders to him that he had wrought and yet used no rarer spell than a certain wave of his arm. She spoke of the magical orchids that came down once over cliffs like a sudden roseate foam breaking over the Elfin Mountains. She spoke of the downy clusters of queer mauve flowers which bloomed in the grass of the dells, and of that glory of blossom that forever guarded the lawns. For all these wonders were his: bird-song and blooming of flower alike were his inspirations. If such wonders as song and bloom were wrought by a wave of his hand, surely he might by beckoning bring but a short way from Earth some few fields that lay so near to the earthly border. Or surely he might move Elfland a little earthward again, who had lately moved it as far as the turn in the path of the comet, and had brought it again to the edge of the fields of men.

"Never," he said, "can any rune but one, or spell or wonder or any magical thing, move our realm one wing's width over the earthly border or bring anything thence here. And little they know in those fields that even one rune can do it."

And still she would scarce believe that those accustomed powers of her wizard sire could not easily bring the things of Earth and the wonders of Elfland together.

"From those fields," he said, "my spells are all beaten back, my incantations are mute, and my right arm powerless."

And when he spoke thus to her of that dread right arm, at last perforce she believed him. And she prayed him again for that ultimate rune, that long-hoarded treasure of Elfland, that potency that had strength to work against the harsh weight of Earth.

And his thoughts went into the future all alone, peering far down the years. More gladly had a traveller at night in lonely ways given up his lantern than had this elvish king now used his last great spell, and so cast it away, and gone without it into those dubious years; whose dim forms he saw and many of their events, but not to the end. Easily had she asked for that dread spell, which should appease the only need she had, easily might he have granted it were he but human; but his vast wisdom saw so much of the years to be that he feared to face them without this last great potency.

"Beyond our border," he said, "material things stand fierce and strong and many, and have the power to darken and to increase, for they have wonders too. And when this last potency be used and gone there remains in all our realm no rune that they dread; and material things will multiply and put the powers in bondage, and we without any rune of which they go in awe shall become no more than a fable. We must yet store this rune."

Thus he reasoned with her rather than commanded, though he was the founder and King of all those lands, and all that wandered in them and of the light in which they shone. And reason in Elfland was no daily thing, but an exotic wonder. With this he sought to soothe her earthward fancies.

And Lirazel made no answer but only wept, weeping tears of enchanted dew. And all the line of the Elfin Mountains quivered, as wandering winds will tremble to notes of a violin that have strayed beyond hearing down the ways of the air; and all the creatures of fable that dwelt in the realm of Elfland felt something strange in their hearts like the dying away of a song.

"Is it not best for Elfland that I do this?" said the King.

And still she only wept.

And then he sighed and considered the welfare of Elfland again. For Elfland drew its happiness from the calm of that palace, which was its centre, and of which only song may tell; and now its spires were troubled and the light of its walls was dim, and a sorrow was floating from its vaulted doorway all over the fields of faery and over the dells of dream. If she were happy Elfland might bask again in that untroubled light and eternal calm whose radiance blesses all but material things; and though his treasury were open and empty yet what more were needed then?

So he commanded, and a coffer was brought before him by elfin things, and the knight of his guard who had watched over it forever came marching behind them.

He opened the coffer with a spell, for it opened to no key, and taking from it an ancient parchment scroll he rose and read from it while his daughter wept. And the words of the rune as he read were like the notes of a band of violins, all played by masters chosen from many ages, hidden on midsummer's midnight in a wood, with a strange moon shining, the air all full of madness and mystery; and, lurking close but invisible, things beyond the wisdom of man.

Thus he read that rune, and powers heard and obeyed it, not alone in Elfland but over the border of Earth.

Chapter XXXIII

The Shining Line

Alveric wandered on, alone of that small company of three without a hope to guide him. For Niv and Zend, who were lately led by the hope of their fantastic quest, no longer yearned for Elfland but were guided now by their plan to hold Alveric back from it. They vacillated more slowly than sane folk, but clung with far more than sane fervour to each vacillation. And Zend that had wandered through so many years with the hope of Elfland before him looked on it, now that he had seen its frontier, as one of the rivals of the moon. Niv who had endured as much for Alveric's quest saw in that magical land something more fabulous than was in all his dreams. And now when Alveric attempted lame cajoleries with those swift and ferocious minds he received no more answers from Zend than the curt statement "It is not the will of the moon": while Niv would only reiterate "Have I not dreams enough?"

They were wandering back again past farms that had known them years before. With their old grey tent more tattered they appeared in the twilight, adding a shade to the evening, in fields wherein they and their tent had become a legend. And never was Alveric unwatched by some mad eye, lest he should slip from the camp and come to Elfland and be where dreams were stranger than Niv's and under a power more magical than the moon.

Often he tried, creeping silently from his place in the dead of night. One moonlight night he tried first, waiting awake till all the world seemed sleeping. He knew that the frontier was not far away as he crept from the tent into the brightness and black shadows and passed Niv sleeping heavily. A little way he went, and there was Zend sitting still on a rock, gazing into the face of the moon. Round came Zend's face and, newly inspired by the moon, he shouted and leapt at Alveric. They had taken away his sword. And Niv woke and came towards them with immense fury, united to Zend by one jealousy; for each of them knew well that the wonders of Elfland were greater than any fancy that their minds would ever know.

And again he tried, on a night when no moon shone. But on that night Niv was sitting outside the camp, relishing in a strange and joyless way a certain comradeship that there was between his ravings and the interstellar darkness. And there in the night he saw Alveric slipping away towards the land whose wonders far transcended all Niv's poor dreams; and all the fury the lesser can feel for the greater awoke at once in his mind; and, creeping up behind him, without any help from Zend he smote Alveric insensible to the ground.

And never did Alveric plan any escape after that but that the busy thoughts of madness anticipated it.

And so they came, watchers and watched, over the fields of men. And Alveric sought help of the folk of the farms; but the cunning of Niv knew too well the tricks of sanity. So that when the folk came running over their fields to that queer grey tent from which they heard Alveric's cries, they found Niv and Zend posed in a calm that they had much practised, while Alveric told of his thwarted quest of Elfland. Now by many men all quests are considered mad, as the cunning of Niv knew. Alveric found no help here.

As they went back by the way by which they had marched for years Niv led that band of three, stepping ahead of Alveric and Zend with his lean face held high, made all the leaner by the long thin points to which he had trained his beard and his moustaches, and wearing Alveric's sword that stuck out long behind him and its hilt high in front. And he stepped and perked his head with a certain air that revealed to the rare travellers who saw him that this sparse and ragged figure esteemed itself the leader of a greater band than were visible. Indeed if one had just seen him at the end of the evening with the dusk and the mist of the fenlands close behind him he might have believed that in the dusk and the mist was an army that followed this gay worn confident man. Had the army been there Niv was sane. Had the world accepted that an army was there, even though only Alveric and Zend followed his curious steps, still he was sane. But the lonely fancy that had not fact to feed on, nor the fancy of any other for fellowship, was for its loneliness mad.

Zend watched Alveric all the while, as they marched behind Niv; for their mutual jealousy of the wonders of Elfland bound Niv and Zend together to work as with one wild whim.

And now one morning Niv stretched himself up to the fullest possible height of his lean inches and extended his right arm high and addressed his army, "We are come near again to Erl," he said. "And we shall bring new fancies in place of outworn things and things that are stale; and its customs shall be henceforth the way of the moon."

Now Niv cared nothing for the moon, but he had great cunning, and he knew that Zend would aid his new plan against Erl if only for the sake of the moon. And Zend cheered till the echoes came back from a lonely hill, and Niv smiled to them like a leader confident of his hosts. And Alveric rose against them then, and struggled with Niv and Zend for the last time, and learned that age or wandering or loss of hope had left him unable to strive against the maniacal strength of these two. And after that he went with them more meekly, with resignation, caring no longer what befell him, living only in memory and only for days that had been; and in November evenings in this dim camp in the chill he saw, looking only backwards through the years, Spring mornings shine again on the towers of Erl. In the light of these mornings he saw Orion again, playing again with old toys that the witch had made with a spell; he saw Lirazel move once more through the gracious gardens. Yet no light that memory is able to kindle was strong enough to illumine much that camp in those sombre evenings, when the damp rose up from the ground and the chill swooped out of the air, and Niv and Zend as darkness came stealing nearer began to chatter in low eager voices schemes inspired by such whims as throve at dusk in the waste. Only when the sad day drifted wholly thence and Alveric slept by flapping tatters that streamed from the tent in the night, then only was memory, unhindered by the busy changes of day, able to bring back Erl to him, bright, happy and vernal; so that while his body lay still, in far fields, in the dark and the Winter, all that was most active and live in him was back over the wolds in Erl, back over the years in Spring with Lirazel and Orion.

How far he was bodily, in sheer miles from his home, for which his happy thoughts each night forsook his weary frame, Alveric knew not. It was many years since their tent had stood one evening a grey shape in that landscape in which it now waved its tatters. But Niv knew that of late they had come nearer to Erl, for his dreams of it came to him now soon after he fell asleep, and they used to come to him further on in the night, on the other side of midnight and even towards morning: and from this he argued that they used to have further to come, and were now but a little way off. When he told this secretly one evening to Zend, Zend listened gravely but gave no opinion, merely saying "The moon knows." Nevertheless he followed Niv, who led this curious caravan always in that direction from which his dreams of the valley of Erl came soonest. And this queer leadership brought them nearer to Erl, as often happens where men follow leaders that are crazy or blind or deceived; they reach some port or other though they stray down the years with little foresight enough: were it otherwise what would become of us?

And one day the upper parts of the towers of Erl looked at them out of blue distance, shining in early sunlight above a curve of the downs. And towards them Niv turned at once and led directly, for the line of their wandering march had not pointed straight to Erl, and marched on as a conqueror that sees some new city's gates. What his plans were Alveric did not know, but kept to his apathy; and Zend did not know, for Niv had merely said that his plans must be secret; nor did Niv know, for his fancies poured through his brain and rushed away; what fancies made what plans in a mood that was yesterday's how could he tell to-day?

Then as they went they soon came to a shepherd, standing amongst his grazing sheep and leaning upon his crook, who watched and seemed to have no other care but only to watch all things going by, or, when nothing passed, to gaze and gaze at the downs till all his memories were fashioned out of their huge grass curves. He stood, a bearded man, and watched them with never a word as they passed. And one of Niv's mad memories suddenly knew him, and Niv hailed him by his name and the shepherd answered. And who should he be but Vand!

Then they fell talking; and Niv spoke suavely, as he always did with sane folk, aping with clever mimicry the ways and the tricks of sanity, lest Alveric should ask for help against him. But Alveric sought no help. Silent he stood and heard the others talking, but his thoughts were far in the past and their voices were only sounds to him. And Vand enquired of them if they had found Elfland. But he spoke as one asks of children if their toy boat has been to the Happy Isles. He had had for many years to do with sheep, and had come to know their needs and their price, and the need men have of them; and these things had risen imperceptibly up all round his imagination, and were at last a wall over which he saw no further. When he was young, yes once, he had sought for Elfland; but now, why now he was older; such things were for the young.

"But we saw its border," said Zend, "the border of twilight."

"A mist," said Vand, "of the evening."

"I have stood," said Zend, "upon the edge of Elfland."

But Vand smiled and shook his bearded head as he leaned on his long crook, and every wave of his beard as he shook it slowly denied Zend's tales of that border, and his lips smiled it away, and his tolerant eyes were grave with the lore of the fields we know.

"No, not Elfland," he said.

And Niv agreed with Vand, for he watched his mood, studying the ways of sanity. And they spoke of Elfland lightly, as one tells of some dream that came at dawn and went away before waking. And Alveric heard with despair, for Lirazel dwelt not only over the border but even, as he saw now, beyond human belief; so that all at once she seemed remoter than ever, and he still lonelier.

"I sought for it once," said Vand, "but no, there's no Elfland."

"No," said Niv, and only Zend wondered.

"No," replied Vand and shook his head and lifted his eyes to his sheep.

And just beyond his sheep and coming towards them he saw a shining line. So long his eyes stayed fixed on that shining line coming over the downs from the eastward that the others turned and looked.

They saw it too, a shimmering line of silver, or a little blue like steel, flickering and changing with the reflection of strange passing colours. And before it, very faint like threatening breezes breathing before a storm, came the soft sound of very old songs. It caught, as they all stood gazing, one of Vand's furthest sheep; and instantly its fleece was that pure gold that is told of in old romance; and the shining line came on and the sheep disappeared altogether. They saw now that it was about the height of the mist from a small stream; and still Vand stood gazing at it, neither moving nor thinking. But Niv turned very soon and beckoned curtly to Zend and seized Alveric by the arm and hastened away towards Erl. The gleaming line, that seemed to bump and stumble over every unevenness of the rough fields, came not so fast as they hastened; yet it never stopped when they rested, never wearied when they were tired, but came on over all the hills and hedges of Earth; nor did sunset change its appearance or check its pace.

Chapter XXXIV

The Last Great Rune

As Alveric hastened back, led by two madmen, to those lands over which he had long ago been lord, the horns of Elfland had sounded in Erl all day. And though only Orion heard them, they no less thrilled the air, flooding it deep with their curious golden music, and filling the day with a wonder that others felt; so that many a young girl leaned from her window to see what was enchanting the morning. But as the day wore on the enchantment of the unheard music dwindled, giving place to a feeling that weighed on all minds in Erl and seemed to bode the imminence of some unknown region of wonder. All his life Orion had heard these horns blowing at evening except upon days on which he had done ill: if he heard the horns at evening he knew that it was well with him. But now they had blown in the morning, and blew all day, like a fanfare in front of a march; and Orion looked out of his window and saw nothing, and the horns rang on, proclaiming he knew not what. Far away they called his thoughts from the things of Earth that are the concern of men, far away from all that casts shadows. He spoke to no man that day, but went among his trolls and such elfin things as had followed them over the border. And all men that saw him perceived such a look in his eyes as showed his thoughts to be far in realms that they dreaded. And his thoughts were indeed far thence, once more with his mother. And hers were with him, lavishing tendernesses that the years had denied her, in their swift passage over our fields that she never had understood. And somehow he knew she was nearer.

And all that strange morning the will-o'-the-wisps were restless and the trolls leaped wildly all about their lofts, for the horns of Elfland tinged all the air with magic and excited their blood although they could not hear them. But towards evening they felt impending some great change and all grew silent and moody. And something brought to them yearnings for their far magical home, as though a breeze had blown suddenly into their faces straight off the tarns of Elfland; and they ran up and down the street looking for something magical, to ease their loneliness amongst mundane things. But found nothing resembling the spell-born lilies that grew in their glory above the elfin tarns. And the folk of the village perceived them everywhere and longed for the wholesome earthly days again that there were before the coming of magic to Erl. And some of them hurried off to the house of the Freer and took refuge with him amongst his holy things from all the unhallowed shapes that there were in their streets and all the magic that tingled and loomed in the air. And he guarded them with his curses which floated away the light and almost aimless will-o'-the-wisps, and even, at a short distance, awed the trolls, but they ran and capered only a little way off. And while the little group clustered about the Freer, seeking solace from him against whatever impended, with which the air was growing tenser and grimmer as the short day wore on, there went others to Narl and the busy elders of Erl to say "See what your plans have done. See what you have brought on the village."

And none of the elders made immediate answer, but said that they must take counsel one with another, for they trusted greatly in the words said in their parliament. And to this intent they gathered again at the forge of Narl. It was evening now, but the sun had not yet set nor Narl gone from his work, but his fire was beginning to glow with a deeper colour among the shadows that had entered his forge. And the elders came in there walking slowly with grave faces, partly because of the mystery that they needed to cover their folly from the sight of the villagers, partly because magic hung now so gross in the air that they feared the imminence of some portentous thing. They sat in their parliament in that inner room, while the sun went low and the elfin horns, had they but known it, blew clear and triumphantly. And there they sat in silence, for what could they say? They had wished for magic, and now it had come. Trolls were in all the streets, goblins had entered houses, and now the nights were mad with will-o'-the-wisps; and all the air was heavy with unknown magic. What could they say? And after a while Narl said they must make a new plan; for they had been plain bell-fearing folk, but now there were magical things all over Erl, and more came every night from Elfland to join them, and what would become of the old ways unless they made a plan?

And Narl's words emboldened them all, though they felt the ominous menace of the horns that they could not hear; but the talk of a plan emboldened them, for they deemed they could plan against magic. And one by one they rose to speak of a plan.

But at sunset the talk died down. And their dread that something impended grew now to a certain knowledge. Oth and Threl knew it first, who had lived familiar with mystery in the woods. All knew that something was coming. No one knew what. And they all sat silent wondering in the gloaming.

Lurulu saw it first. He had dreamed all day of the weed-green tarns of Elfland, and growing weary of Earth, had gone all lonely to the top of a tower that rose from the Castle of Erl and perched himself on a battlement and gazed wistfully homewards. And looking out over the fields we know, he saw the shining line coming down on Erl. And from it he heard rise faint, as it rippled over the furrows, a murmur of many old songs; for it came with all manner of memories, old music and lost voices, sweeping back again to our old fields what time had driven from Earth. It was coming towards him bright as the Evening Star, and flashing with sudden colours, some common on Earth, and some unknown to our rainbow; so that Lurulu knew it at once for the frontier of Elfland. And all his impudence returned to him at sight of his fabulous home, and he uttered shrill gusts of laughter from his high perch, that rang over the roofs below like the chatter of building birds. And the little homesick trolls in the lofts were cheered by the sound of his merriment though they knew not from what it came. And now Orion heard the horns blowing so loud and near, and there was such triumph in their blowing, and pomp, and withal so wistful a crooning, that he knew now why they blew, knew that they proclaimed the approach of a princess of the elfin line, knew that his mother came back to him.

High on her hill Ziroonderel knew this, being forwarned by magic; and looking downward at evening she saw that star-like line of blended twilights of old lost Summer evenings sweeping over the fields towards Erl. Almost she wondered as she saw this glittering thing flowing over the earthly pastures, although her wisdom had told her that it must come. And on the one side she saw the fields we know, full of accustomed things, and on the other, looking down from her height, she saw, behind the myriad-tinted border, the deep green elfin foliage and Elfland's magical flowers, and things that delirium sees not, nor inspiration, on Earth; and the fabulous creatures of Elfland prancing forward; and, stepping across our fields and bringing Elfland with her, the twilight flowing from both her hands, which she stretched out a little from her, was her own lady the Princess Lirazel coming back to her home. And at this sight, and at all the strangeness coming across our fields, or because of old memories that came with the twilight or bygone songs that sang in it, a strange joy came shivering upon Ziroonderel, and if witches weep she wept.

And now from upper windows of the houses the folk began to see that glittering line which was no earthly twilight: they saw it flash at them with its starry gleam and then flow on towards them. Slowly it came as though it rippled with difficulty over Earth's rugged bulk, though moving lately over the rightful lands of the Elf King it had outspeeded the comet. And hardly had they wondered at its strangeness, when they found themselves amongst most familiar things, for the old memories that floated before it, as a wind before the thunder, beat in a sudden gust on their hearts and their houses, and lo! they were living once more amongst things long past and lost. And as that line of no earthly light came nearer there rustled before it a sound as of rain on leaves, old sighs, breathed over again, old lovers' whispers repeated. And there fell on these folk as they all leaned hushed from their windows a mood that looked gently, wistfully backward through time, such a mood as might lurk by huge dock-leaves in ancient gardens when everyone is gone that has tended their roses or ever loved the bowers.

Not yet had that line of starlight and bygone loves lapped at the walls of Erl or foamed on the houses, but it was so near now that already there slipped away the daily cares that held folk down to the present, and they felt the balm of past days and blessings from hands long withered. Now elders ran out to children that skipped with a rope in the street, to bring them into the houses, not telling them why, for fear of frightening their daughters. And the alarm in their mothers' faces for a moment startled the children; then some of them looked to the eastward and saw that shining line. "It is Elfland coming," they said, and went on with their skipping.

And the hounds knew, though what they knew I cannot say; but some influence reached them from Elfland such as comes from the full moon, and they bayed as they bay on clear nights when the fields are flooded with moonlight. And the dogs in the streets that always watched lest anything strange should come, knew how great a strangeness was near them now and proclaimed it to all the valley.

Already the old leather-worker in his cottage across the fields, looking out of his window to see if his well were frozen, saw a May morning of fifty years ago and his wife gathering lilac, for Elfland had beaten Time away from his garden.

And now the jackdaws had left the towers of Erl and flew away westward; and the baying of the hounds filled all the air, and the barking of lesser dogs. This suddenly ceased and a great hush fell on the village, as though snow had suddenly fallen inches deep. And through the hush came softly a strange old music; and no one spoke at all.

Then where Ziroonderel sat by her door with her chin on her hand gazing, she saw the bright line touch the houses and stop, flowing past them on either side but held by the houses, as though it had met with something too strong for its magic; but for only a moment the houses held back that wonderful tide, for it broke over them with a burst of unearthly foam, like a meteor of unknown metal burning in heaven, and passed on and the houses stood all quaint and queer and enchanted, like homes remembered out of a long-past age by the sudden waking of an inherited memory.

And then she saw the boy she had nursed step forward into the twilight, drawn by a power no less than that which was moving Elfland: she saw him and his mother meet again in all that light that was flooding the valley with splendour. And Alveric was with her, he and she together a little apart from attendant fabulous things, that escorted her all the way from the vales of the Elfin Mountains. And from Alveric had fallen away that heavy burden of years, and all the sorrow of wandering: he too was back again in the days that were, with old songs and lost voices. And Ziroonderel could not see the princess's tears when she met Orion again after all that separation of space and time, for, though they flashed like stars, she stood in the border in all that radiance of starlight that shone about her like the broad face of a planet. But though the witch saw not this there came to her old ears clearly the sounds of songs returning again to our fields out of the glens of Elfland, wherein they had lain so long, which were all the old songs lost from the nurseries of the Earth. They crooned now about the meeting of Lirazel and Orion.

And Niv and Zend had ease at last from their fierce fancies, for their wild thoughts sank to rest in the calm of Elfland and slept as hawks sleep in their trees when evening has lulled the world. Ziroonderel saw them standing together where the edge of the downs had been, a little way off from Alveric. And there was Vand amongst his golden sheep, that were munching the strange sweet juices of wonderful flowers.

With all these wonders Lirazel came for her son, and brought Elfland with her that never had moved before the width of a harebell over the earthly border. And where they met was an old garden of roses under the towers of Erl, where once she had walked, and none had cared for it since. Great weeds were now in its walks, and even they were withered with the rigour of late November: their dry stalks hissed about his feet as Orion walked through them, and they swung back brown behind him over untended paths. But before him bloomed in all their glory and beauty the great voluptuous roses gorgeous with Summer. Between November that she was driving before her and that old season of roses that she brought back to her garden Lirazel and Orion met. For a moment the withered garden lay brown behind him, then it all flashed into bloom, and the wild glad song of birds from a hundred arbours welcomed back the old roses. And Orion was back again in the beauty and brightness of days whose dim fair shades his memory cherished, such as are the chief of all the treasures of man; but the treasury in which they lie is locked, and we have not the key. Then Elfland poured over Erl.

Only the holy place of the Freer and the garden that was about it remained still of our Earth, a little island all surrounded by wonder, like a mountain peak all rocky, alone in air, when a mist wells up in the gloaming from highland valleys, and leaves only one pinnacle darkly to gaze at the stars. For the sound of his bell beat back the rune and the twilight for a little distance all round. There he lived happy, contented, not quite alone, amongst his holy things, for a few that had been cut off by that magical tide lived on the holy island and served him there. And he lived beyond the age of ordinary men, but not to the years of magic.

None ever crossed the boundary but one, the witch Ziroonderel, who from her hill that was just on the earthward border would go by broom on starry nights to see her lady again, where she dwelt unvexed by years, with Alveric and Orion. Thence she comes sometimes, high in the night on her broom, unseen by any down on the earthly fields, unless you chance to notice star after star blink out for an instant as she passes by them, and sits beside cottage doors and tells queer tales, to such as care to have news of the wonders of Elfland. May I hear her again!

And with the last of his world-disturbing runes sent forth, and his daughter happy once more, the elfin King on his tremendous throne breathed and drew in the calm in which Elfland basks; and all his realms dreamed on in that ageless repose, of which deep green pools in summer can barely guess; and Erl dreamed too with all the rest of Elfland and so passed out of all remembrance of men. For the twelve that were of the parliament of Erl looked through the window of that inner room, wherein they planned their plans by the forge of Narl, and, gazing over their familiar lands, perceived that they were no longer the fields we know.

THE END

CPSIA information can be obtained
at www.ICGtesting.com
Printed in the USA
LVHW010733100722
723125LV00005B/413

9 781420 978384